easy stages

Peter Robins is a working journalist who lives in South London. His other work includes the collections of short stories *Undo Your Raincoats and Laugh, Our Hero Has Bad Breath* and *The Gay Touch*; and he is a contributor to the anthologies *Cracks in the Image, On the Line, Messer Rondo* and *Edge City on Two Different Plans*. *Easy Stages* is his first novel.

peter robins

easy stages

First published October 1985 by GMP Publishers Ltd
P O Box 247, London N15 6RW, England.

British Library Cataloguing in Publication Data

Robins, Peter
　　Easy stages.
　　I. Title
823′.914[F]　　　　PR6068.0194

　　ISBN 0-907040-96-9

Typeset by MC Typeset, Chatham, Kent.
Printed and bound by Billing & Sons Ltd, Worcester.

for Michael Rhodes

OUR HEADS no more than a metre apart, we pick among sandwiches in a plastic lunch-box. Shade from a striped umbrella extends along our bodies to my calf muscles and a web of untanned creases at the back of Daniel's knees. Lakewater dribbles from our limbs but evaporates before any pattern can form across the planks. As we relax within our circle of tolerable shade we resemble the hands of some king-size clock. Until Daniel moves we coincide exactly with the 13.51 hours on my digital watch. This idle observation would hardly be entertained by anyone other than a holidaymaker. I enjoy the luxury of registering it.

Daniel, having selected an unsalted tomato sandwich that's already splayed – indeed half-toasted – waves it towards me in admonition. Before nibbling he chides me lightly. My pre-occupation with time – a diagnosis from which I can't dissuade him – should have been stuffed at the back of my wardrobe. He knows that's where I've thrown my lightweight suit and straw panama. Not for the first time today he refers to them as my bourgeois post-colonial kit. I smile, yet refuse to be drawn into that argument again. The early afternoon heat precludes for me any discussion of more than trivialities. I push the lunch-box in his direction with a grunt. Daniel extracts an orange. He peels it with his thumb nail, then flips the zest beyond the sundeck's edge before glancing at me.

– Nothing more to eat? . . . It is that stomach of yours again, Ian? Didn't I suggest to you at breakfast this revulsion of yours is psychosomatic? You are just going to have to accept Asia or go. Oh yes . . . you are going to tell me about your culture shock and the jet-lag. You arrived a week ago. It is India you are trying to fight, not mal du ventre . . .

A punkah that sails above me disturbs the heavier shadows. Finger nails cut more deeply into my sweating palms every hour. Three o'clock.

Four soon. Dawn. The night staff – kitchen and reception and night service too – are generous with promises of chilled pineapple juice. Just where the sodding hell is it, then? Now this must be . . . what? Let's settle for the twelfth or umpteenth time I've flushed the loo. The whole impulsive project has been a mistake. A preposterous whim the size of this subcontinent. Would there have been endless discomfort in Copenhagen? There would not. In the Cliff House Hotel Torquay? Unthinkable. One fact is sure. I shall never be well nor anticipate food or anything else until the damp runways of Heathrow fan out below me.

When it is light and after I have shaved I'll pick my way among the stinking mounds of hooves and trotters with their attendant carrion. Somehow I'll stagger between half-naked toddlers who trail the cows to catch their steaming – do not think of that word – and on to the offices of Air France. My return must be rescheduled. Must be immediate. There has to be one single seat tonight. An end to this ongoing assault and battery by colour, tumult and stench. I need out. Today. If necessary the High Commission must be appealed to and coerced . . .

Why will the sodding night staff not answer the sodding phone?

Out of Delhi. My rupees are dwindling faster – if that is possible – than the loo paper. There'll just not be sufficient (of either would be a safe bet) to see me to Kashmir, with maybe a day's excursion by air-conditioned coach among the Himalayan foothills. I should be stranded – just my luck – in some village without a Consul and with a worse telephone service than this hotel. All a mistake. Better out of this damned country now, with its omnipresent chorus of beggars, touts, taxi-robbers and tarts who converge on every tourist like blowflies in the lobby. And once again – within minutes this time – the battered replica of Rodin's Thinker squats pissing through two holes while cursing a London chemist with his stock of ineffectual lozenges. One dose every four hours.

Absobloodyuseless.

With stinging arse and a dizzy head I creep to the single bed on which the day-shift waiter and I hugged and cuddled to a climax no more than twelve hours – though it could very well be years – ago. Oh yes. This was a trip iridescent with promise for all of one full day.

Having smashed the phone into what feels like its cradle, I thump the bedside light-switch with my fist. And do I care a (not that word) if some sleeping family trembles in a neighbouring room at my manic performance? Not even a damn. I grab the lozenge carton one last time. Would it be practical to sue my chemist under the Trades Description Act? I reread the instructions – not silently but in a fury. Every syllable is shouted with deliberate emphasis.

My shriek of laughter might summon even sleeping waiters. This outburst could be more effective than the phone. Families on either side of me – even the floor below – are most probably packing and ready to evacuate. I am weeping with laughter. Not one miserable tablet four times a day. Four bloody tablets four times a day. I shake six brown bombers into an unsteady palm. What the hell if I become a State Registered Morphine Addict? And do I care if the chilled drinking water in my thermos has long since been guzzled? Do I hell. One lozenge to one mouthful of tapwater. This is my holiday and mean-minded or not I am going to ENJOY it. Goodbye the well-meant guide book strictures. Forget those bottles of mineral water in which Nanny advises one should always brush one's teeth .

Tomorrow I shall breakfast on unwashed nectarines and dine on risky water-ices. Forget all this bystanding at an antiseptic distance. Line up the Himalayan shepherds while I doze back to health. Tomorrow I'll be among those lithe boatmen who cruise across the covers of every brochure that invites us to Kashmir's lakes. Prote refreshed by sleep will be himself again and talent-spotting within hours.

– Give over with the sales chat, Daniel. You're not briefing one of your white-kneed groups now. Listen, will you? The only thing I'm battling against is the way all the food – and that includes this tacky lunch – is thrown together and chucked at us. That's my only gripe. Be honest now. This unappetising muck would hardly attract a ravenous adolescent, would it . . ?

– Or the starving in Calcutta? Can you really swear to me Ian that you weren't anticipating some floating Hilton? Some cheap high-living provided by breadline labour costs?

– Oh come on . . .

– Well, many of my Americans suppose that is exactly what they will find. I have to tell them it is no use stamping around doing an angry Caucasian dance. This is the Third World. Are you sure you're not being post-imperialist again?

– Don't preach. I'm not forgetting Calcutta. Or Delhi. Decently curried beans and a tub of yoghurt would be quite acceptable. That's all I'm asking. We are staying on what's billed as a super-de-luxe houseboat. Had you overlooked the prices they're charging? *You* certainly should be pampered with VIP treatment. One adverse report from a regular guide like yourself and that mafiosi of a management would have its contract shredded to confetti by tour operators . . .

I meander towards the grumbling conclusion that our

houseboat – far from offering a lakeside loll – is fundamentally no more than Assembly Point and Base Camp One for Himalayan trekkers. How else can the unimaginative and unvaried menu be explained? As I stare towards the willows on the horizon, attempting to pick out our landing-stage among a dozen others, I realise I could also have been caustic about the offhand service.

Daniel's smile begins from the pupils of his eyes. Smoothly it extends to include a wrinkling of his nose and then a rapid twitching of his lips. I too begin to laugh at myself. Being genuinely hungry, I select the most pliable of the remaining cucumber sandwiches. When Daniel wipes a smudge of orange juice from his chin, he uses the back of his hand and I notice what is best described as an awesome black bruise. A stripe extending from the heel of his palm to the tips of the two smaller fingers. Before I can comment on this, he folds his arms and slips full-length onto his stomach to scrutinise me.

– Now surely you must have considered going on a gentle hike yourself? How are you going to face your family and all your friends without having really been into the Himalayas?

– Daniel . . .

–Wait. I know you would like to put down what I'm saying as mysticism and nonsense . . . but I wish you would believe me. The solitude up there is an experience every person should have . . .

– Hmmm . . .

– There would be no need to go deep into Zanskar. You would find even the bus journey up to Leh quite exhilarating. Do you understand, Ian, what I am talking about? It has nothing to do with Buddhism or a passion for geology or what you laugh about as Boy Scouting . . .

Beyond Daniel's prone body and the deck of the swimming-boat the lake spreads round us like a sheet of beaten brass. Further still – beyond poplars that fringe the north shore – foothills begin. Without raising my head I can observe ravines camouflaged, even now in August, by deep packs of ice. It is not only Daniel who urges me to quit the shady corner of our boat's verandah where I read each afternoon. I am irritated daily by the probings of boatmen who float me in a shikara on a ritual sundown cruise. Their questions and suggestions intrude as I scan the shore road, then each passing craft, for one interesting face. If it is not the services of their younger brothers they are offering, then it is their brothers-in-law who will be delighted to drive me to the glaciers in some borrowed clapped-out jeep.

During every meal our waiters – not disinterestedly – enquire who will be leaving when for Pahalgam or Kargil. Wherever they may be. All I've gleaned of Kargil from returning travellers is that the town is seemingly lit by candles every night between eight and eleven. The tourists, having eaten, return to beds where the bugs wait impatiently to perform their harvest dance.

The persuasiveness of fellow guests leaves me unmoved. More exactly, it augments my obduracy as it would were team games being organised. It must be conceded that Daniel is no commonplace hearty, urging quiet bystanders – well, I mean me – to conformity. Possibly the secrets of those hidden valleys which so obviously delight him are not lightly shared month in, month out with transitory groups. I wonder how easily he manages to accept the crass questioning of package tourists as the price he must pay for his freedom, between assignments, to explore a landscape of private streams which gush – or so he tells me – across the uncharted rooftops of our world.

I finish chewing a miniscule banana while folding the skin neatly into the shell of a hard-boiled egg.

– Daniel . . . I may go and take a look for myself. In my own good time. I suspect you don't believe I'd no grand purpose in coming to India . . .

– Now why should you say . . ?

– Okay. If you want a laugh, let me admit I didn't even skim one bloody guidebook before I left London. Glanced at one brochure in the plane. Now some of your more devoted trippers – well, they may have been some of yours for all I know – stagger back as though they'd been on a pilgrimage. Weighed down with sacred relics they are. Prayer wheels for Sydney and carvings for Ottawa. And there's almost a – well, a *smugness* in their glance. A quest completed . . .

– And you include me?

– No. But I do include Miles who seems to be acting as a guide. He really is a stereotype of my countrymen at their most laughable. Have you ever watched him strutting round the houseboat last thing at night? He's like some cut-out hero from a war film in love with his own farts. Now Miles would view each mountain trek as a keep-fit exercise to ward off decadence.

– That's what he's told you?

– Not exchanged a syllable with him since I arrived. But that's

what he *would* say, I know. He'd assure me I would return from
the passes up there a fitter man. For what I can't imagine . . .

– *Why aren't you up, Ian, and out for an early morning run with Miles
instead of lopping about in bed reading?*

– *Thank you stepfather . . . surely the war's been over some time
now? Seems more practical for my generation to exercise the mind . . .*

– *No healthy mind without a healthy body. You'll never convince
me, young man, that novels can extend any fifteen-year-old . . . The
war may be over but you'll both be facing conscription soon enough. A
lad in good shape always achieves a commission more easily. Your
mother – I'm certain I can speak for her in this – would be upset if her
son remained a mere squaddie in the Infantry.*

– *Will you let me worry about that, please? If Miles wishes to be an
officer – and a gentleman – that's his business. And yours. As for me
I may very well decide to be a poet . . .*

– *Hardly a manly occupation, Ian. And – if I may say so – not one
that is very well paid. Your father didn't exactly leave . . .*

– *Forgive me stepfather, but I've gathered from what I've read –
what I've heard you say in the pulpit too – that the founder of your
profession didn't rate manliness or money that highly. Come to that, I
could be a pacifist too. Like him . . .*

– *That's as near blasphemy as I wish to hear before celebrating
Eucharist. I shall ask your mother to clear the table. You'll have to fend
for yourself when you finally leave this sty of yours . . .*

Daniel's attention began to drift before I'd made a second
satirical observation about Miles. While I was recollecting a
Sunday morning long ago – or one fragment of it – he was
refocussing on two women who were settling in chairs on the
deck of a swimming-boat to the starboard of our own.

At the nape Daniel's hair is baby soft. This contrasts
remarkably with the skin on his neck that has been weathered to
dark suede. Whether he has accepted my scepticism about the
mystical experiences thrown in as a bonus with mountain-
trekking, I can't know. When he leans forward I suspect that
what he's about to tell me would have been said had I stayed
silent.

– There's really no mountaineering skill involved, Ian. Up
there you can walk almost as effortlessly as we strolled into
town this morning.

– You're having me on . . .

– No. Well, perhaps near Leh it can be strenuous from time to

12

time, but any good guide will always pause for the last person in his group to catch up. I'm sure even Miles does that. Sometime you must tell me why you so dislike him . . .

– Maybe. You were saying?

– I was about to say again that my argument isn't based on religion. It has everything to do with the need people have to come face-to-face with themselves. Can they do that in the middle of Paris or London or New York?

– One might try . . .

– And fail. It is too easy to turn on the television or pick up the phone. In the mountains, when you've broken camp after breakfast you must walk alone at your own pace before the lunch stop. It has to be. There's so little spare energy for chatter at that altitude. Now. Let's apply all that to you. What have you to fear from the physical demands anyway? You're built for long distances. When I stopped laughing at that old-fashioned backstroke you were doing before our picnic, I watched your leg movements. Sturdy is the English word, I think? You were a marathon runner?

– All this Gallic flattery will get you nowhere, Daniel. No. Not marathon. Just cross-country stuff and far too long ago to recall much of it . . .

Fifty minutes of Welsh hillside behind me. Five more remain through farms and around cow-pats and over bramble hedges. A tape at the jetty will be unbroken, for there's not one contender over my shoulder. Still no stitch. Ample breath remaining to simulate a spectacular finish. Applause – but of course – from own college supporters and no doubt a couple of photographers ready to record my performance. Applause too (ironic and slower) from Gwyn who – later – will be reticent as always in the shower about tries he's successfully converted while I've been plastering my thighs with mud. Our king-size cheese on toast will taste the sweeter for two halves of lager. Sweetest though, the April evening we'll share on a truckle bed . . .

At dawn Gwyn proposes – a second time – that we should share a flat after finals. There's a silence. I recall that silence. Can just catch, so very faintly still, an eighteen-year-old gulping before he mutters that only peroxided chorus boys live together . . .

About now – dawn British Summer Time – Gwyn's son is stirring. He – on some vacation course or in some tent – will not be so inhibited or so bloody witless, whoever's shoulder he may be stroking gently.

– More to the point, Daniel, I watched you. From your build I'd

13

have guessed you might be happier with short hauls than a ten-day stretch among the glaciers. Well, it just demonstrates we should never construct too much on a single glance.

There's much of the boy athlete about him. A hairless chest and neat pubescent nipples. Even yesterday's stubble on his chin – and he thirty-two or whatever – is no more obvious than the fur on peaches. If I seem to contradict myself within minutes so be it, but I do wonder whether this boyishness might not be evidence of protracted adolescence. Will Daniel continue to trek through the years scoffing canned fish at sunset and declaring it all to be tremendous fun? And the sun up there – unkinder each summer – will it increasingly highlight the lines that have already begun to fringe those cornflower eyes?

This has to be Saturday. As I make the calculation, our unimpeded view of the other swimming-boats and weedpickers plying their overloaded punts is noisily interrupted. Our private chatter and similar murmurings from beneath other shades are lost in shouting and joking. A dozen – nearer fifteen to be accurate – Kashmiris have perched like busy birds along the sundeck's edge. Mostly teenagers. Stripped for swimming they may be. It soon appears they are more eager to loll in the heat, content to display themselves in their gaudy shorts or faded threadbare slips. There's a prolonged comparison of biceps. Incredible energy is expended in miming bullworkers. Their pectorals are unexceptional. This attention to the trappings of machismo evokes memories of Miles.

This – and presumably every – Saturday afternoon the local lads bring to these placid lakes some of the bustle of those markets and noisy alleys beyond the poplars. Daniel is watching not them but me.

– The Kashmiri men consider themselves to be very hand-some. You also use the word macho? What do you think of them, Ian?

If this is some casual opening move, friend Daniel will discover damn all. On his invitation I am here for a picnic and a swim. There'll be no dancing naked on a table for his delight. An impulse to strip down to the soul in public has never been my thing.

Does so protective an irritation betray still – on the very doorstep of middle-age – an oversensitive skin? The hell with it. What reason can there be to swop anything other than holiday commonplaces with this Frenchman? Tomorrow or the next day I'll have difficulty remembering his name, as he will mine. Maybe Daniel enjoys a comfy heart to heart? Possible. Their city suits exchanged for parkas, his adventurous hearties might well give in to some urge to strip. Stimulated by the matiness of the camp-fire, as it were. And Daniel? Does he cast himself as an oak on which they may lean? Well . . . let them enjoy their boyish pleasures. This Parisian, with his glance that seems less complicated than the wayside flowers, owes me nothing and should expect less.

– Not to be too waspish about it, Daniel, they remind me of Groucho Marx playing Valentino. I've not given them any close scrutiny, mind . . .

– But you must have some impression . . .

– Oh yes. I'd say they spend much of their waking lives manoeuvring themselves into the best bargaining positions. They sniff out advantage with noses more prominent than my own. Whether it's offering tourist trash . . . a boat ride . . . sex . . . it's all one long haggle. And every deal has to be clinched with operatic glances and gestures that shouldn't deceive a blind man in a fog . . .

Daniel chokes on the last of the unblemished peaches. Tourists and Kashmiris alike are diverted by his explosive coughs and my back-thumping. When he is breathing more naturally I pass him the remnants of a glass of tepid apple juice.

– Very waspish. Very accurate. No one loves professional traders, eh? The Ladakhi farmers you will meet in Leh – yes, you will go finally, I am sure of it – detest these people very much. Kashmiris are the exploiters. They have the knack of buying cheap in the north at this time of the year. In the winter you will find them plundering what they can from tourists and their fellow countrymen in the south.

– I'm only saying recognise them for what they are. If they weren't on to all the rackets . . . someone else would be. No vacuum.

– Of course. And it is true they give a non-stop performance of the macho male. Do you realise I have to warn any woman who comes trekking that she will be thought by bachelors – like those guys – to be a sex-crazy spinster hunting for an innocent Kashmiri youth?

– Innocent? That lot? A fair few of them haven't merely looked on the sins of the world, they've devised some innovations. Daniel . . . the morning I arrived in Delhi an eight-year-old offered me the juiciest postcards from the Karma Sutra. Three steps on and a twelve-year-old was hawking his sister. He advertised her as very virgin, but when I stared ahead he grabbed my wrist and added that he himself was full of naughty tricks at five rupees an hour.

– You could have seduced them both for the price of a bag of apples . . .

– Watch it, monsieur. Don't try leading me. I accept that on the plains in the south anything and anyone has to be vendable. No. Sod it, I don't accept . . .

– Moral principles?

– Bollockchops. I don't accept it because here in the Vale of Kashmir the land's as lush and fertile as any hectare back in France. Oh you know it's true! And what's more, I hear that in the four-star hotel over there every dining-table is packed with India's new bourgeoisie – the Intermediate Class the buggers call themselves – I see you've heard of them too. Let's hear more about the inequalities India is perpetuating for herself before we hand round any more pamphlets back home about kids with Belsen eyes. . .

– That is harsh but I have to admit there's some basis in what you say. You should also understand, Ian, that they have this sense of karma . . . the beggers and the untouchables accept it is their destiny to be impoverished. . .

– Oh bugger the karma. Let's get the calories right first . . .

The two women on the next swimming-boat are steadying each other on the shiny wooden steps while water laps across their ankles. One wears a plain navy swimming-costume. Her black hair is trimmed *en brosse*. Her friend pointing at the lake surface is probably indicating the shoals of small fish that wait expectantly for crumbs. (Does a fish have a sense of karma?) The second woman wears a flowery bikini and her matching headscarf conceals all but one of her clouded honey ringlets. The young Kashmiris are also assessing these women. The nudges, if not the whispered comments, are comprehensible. On any crowded Mediterranean beach or in a city pool who'd notice just two more women about to swim? Here above the stillness of Dal Lake they instantly become a focus of attention. Their movements disturb the baked air. Even a power-boat that laced the water from the shore to shore before we ate has now been moored. The skier who tumbled a couple of times in its wake seemed – from this hundred metres distance – to resemble Miles.

Perhaps I supposed it to be Miles for my private amusement?

I call to the women between cupped hands.

– Watch that muck on the step below the waterline . . . you'll skid on your backs.

Supplementary information from Daniel evokes laughter from the multinational group of spectators.

– And those little fishes around your toes . . . They might not be minnows . . . My friend suspects they could be piranas . . .

The women laugh at this and wave their thanks before the dark-haired one dives. She splits the water with a professional grace. I register this as I consider Daniel's first public reference to me as his friend. Is he setting up a Two Of Us and Two Of You situation? It doesn't astound me that he asks quietly if I find the two women attractive. Surely he can't suppose I'll instantly come out with a declaration of my private preferences? If that was his ploy my answer must disappoint him. I tell him – a little ambiguously – that our definitions of attractiveness may not coincide, but I do add I'd be delighted to meet the two women for a drink. To deter him from any further work on a cosy script for the four of us, I suggest it could be interesting to hear a woman's view of Kashmir and the Kashmiris. Not only the males. Since Daniel appears to be waiting for me to expand on this, I conclude:

– I'm no sexual pirana, Daniel.

He turns away a moment to contemplate the blonde who lingers in the afternoon heat, content to swim her toe round the surface of the lake. She may be playing tag with the minnows. There is an almost nervous smile round his mouth when he turns back to me again.

– A moment ago I spoke of you as my friend without asking your permission . . . You shrug, Ian. I was not just using a phrase. I think you are a friend because we appear to have more in common than might be expected between two people who have known one another for only a few hours. I am not a predator either for every woman who passes. Like you, I wish to know something of those two as people. Of course . . . I don't deny that beautiful women do fascinate me . . .

As Daniel opens his tobacco-pouch I watch him cautiously. Ten pounds to a penny this conversation is going to linger on relationships. The setting and the time suggest it. This is the moment when picnic crumbs have been gathered up. The hour before the heat of the afternoon falters. In more temperate climates – English commons or shaded backwaters along the Thames or Avon – lovers now move closer. The surer first, then the more timid partner, extends a forearm to conquer that great space which hitherto has been a no man's land between them.

Fumbling for my cigarette pack, I think for the first time since Heathrow dropped away of current lovers with whom I'd willingly share this next half-hour. Squinting across my lighter's flame, I notice again the premature wrinkles in Daniel's forehead and the early crow's feet underneath his eyes. Is it merely the fierce light bouncing from the glaciers that causes him to screw up his features? I begin to wonder if there might be some unresolved personal tensions of which his habit might be a symptom.

– So, Ian my friend . . . Shall we make some attempt to get to know these two women? On the other hand they may prefer the company of Kashmiris. It is not unknown . . . and there is a third possibility . . .

– Only three?

So what is the third? It can't be difficult for Daniel to guess the word feminist is common to both our languages. He didn't use it. His unstated alternative was allowed to drift into suggestiveness. Friend Daniel risks a slap on the wrist. A little obtuseness might flush him out.

– You mean they might be married, Daniel? While the pair of them frolic here like latter-day memsahibs, their poor husbands are slaving over an expenses lunch in some Bombay restaurant, doing their best for Wall Street shareholders or Mother England's export hopes?

It's doubtful whether my improvised fantasy will convince Daniel. Certainly it won't deter him. Both women, I notice, are now crawling round the margin of a lotus garden that has established itself at the stern of their swimming-boat. The ease with which they swim suggests they could be Australian.

– That is an example of your English irony, Ian? I cannot think you are that naif – you also say naif? I was wondering if these two women might be happy without any men at all. The word we use . . .

– We say lesbian, Daniel. If that's what you are suggesting. Forgetting my caution about deceptive appearances? We can all play guessing games. I'm going to bet you've no interest in the dark-haired one . . .

– Correct.

– Because of her hairstyle? Because it's short and boyish?

– And that is precisely why . . .

– Hold it. You of all people here today should have considered she may have had it cropped for easy management in the mountains. She'd be hard put to find a stylist up there. Unless one of your sherpas happened to have trained in a Paris salon. Perhaps she's also aiming to fend off the local lusties.

– But in jeans and a shirt . . ? I mean, if we invite her for a drink tonight, in the dark people might think she's a man . . .

– So? Call it protective clothing as I suggested . . .

The pipe stem is being jabbed directly at my chest. Daniel is uninterested in any explanation but his own.

– Or Ian . . . or . . . her hairstyle and the way she took the lead down those steps and into the water might be her way of proposing to her blonde friend something she does not dare put into words.

– That's a cartload of old cobblers and you know it. Such old world romanticism in a Parisian. I shall call you Danny boy for the rest of the day. Now listen. Anyone self–assured enough to strike out from the hard–worn tourist track . . . Benidorm say . . . or Florida . . . and anyone well-heeled enough to travel as far as they must have done, isn't going to burn his or her lips in silence when it comes to sexual preference. Come on now, Danny. You – a Frenchman – unaware of sexual liberation . . .

– You may be right.

The heat is too enervating for me to bother to exhume Oscar Wilde yet again or to remind him of the *Code Napoléon*. We both relax with a laugh. Or so it seems. Daniel crumbles a savoury biscuit in his left palm but the circular movements of his fingers are anything but relaxed. Manic would be the most exact word. He explains the crumbs are for the birds. Three bulbuls have settled attentively on the back of my unoccupied camp chair. Bulbuls have the cheekiness of London sparrows. As I eat breakfast each morning they play grandmother's steps from the window–ledges of the houseboat onto the frames of the dining chairs and from there to the polished cruets. One, two or even three will perch quite unflummoxed as I snap toast and push the crumbs steadily along the walnut table with a fork. I withdraw the fork to watch and wait. Not for long. They snatch the food with a noisy flurry. Here too – on our boat deck – they are delighted by a mid-afternoon snack and peck at the powdered biscuit less than a metre from Daniel's toes. In no more than a minute they've gobbled the lot.

Both of us slew round so that our scorching legs are shaded from the direct sun. It interests me that this mutual decision of ours was not verbalised. I've noted before that two people – having shared any extended period solely in each other's company – can rapidly begin to rediscover the rudiments of telepathy. The reason for their proximity must never be discounted – a relaxed holiday mood will always be more conducive than being trapped in a lift. Anyway, Daniel and I – more specifically our two heads – face the neighbouring swimming-boat as the two women clamber from the steps to the sundeck. Crop-head beckons a waiter. My hunch is that Daniel won't follow up directly on sexual liberation. But I'm certainly about to be prodded with some indirect questioning. Women in my life?

– So isn't there somebody you ought to be writing to this afternoon, Ian? You did mention Benidorm. We are not in a European playground here, you know. From time to time people do disappear. I mean accidents, of course. You needn't look startled. You are not sharing the afternoon with a psychopath . . .

The smoothness of his tone and the lighthearted pay-off deceive me no more than the blandness of an envelope that conceals unwelcome news or tiresome forms that must be completed. In one sense that is just what Daniel has delivered. A questionnaire, and we're about to start from the top.

Name? Ian Prote. That he knows, or rather that is what I have told him. Address? London would be correct. It is my base, however frequently I travel from it. Occupation? What can I say that might satisfy him? That I sleep for eight hours, that I work – or at least report for work – eight hours each day. Would he be content if I should add that for the remaining third I make meals for friends, make conversation with friends and then make love with one or two I've known for years . . . occasionally with those I've known only for hours? If pressed, how should I define for Daniel the way that I win bread or gain the jam money that's brought me here? Freelance media person it will have to be. Have voice, typewriter and brain for hire to the most agreeable bidder. A nicer kind of arrangement than one would be forced to make in the plains of the south.

Quite clearly the purpose of this coded question is – am I married? What would he deduce from an equally coded answer?

Dear Danny, I have to tell you I am a confirmed and practising bachelor. Having deduced, what would he *do*? Would he take refuge in a heavy bout of pipe-puffing and follow that with a vigorous and cleansing swim until our shikara returns? Later, as we glide towards our houseboat, he might well announce that his dinner plans for the evening will have to be changed. Sorry Ian . . . the tête-à-tête is off. It just so happens one of the sherpa team has arrived and in courtesy they must eat together. Alternatively – and how much more tiresome – Danny might become expansive. Might insist on recounting some incident involving a group he guided a few seasons back.

How would the script run? Evening. Yes, evening and all pretence stripped from the trekkers by the immeasurable silence of the Karocorams. One guy – unmanned without his sportscar and unnerved by the solitude – accuses Daniel of leading them all to perdition. There's a second voice in the twilight. The introspective lad from Brussels or Dublin who's so far been saving his breath to keep pace with the pack. He clasps Daniel tight and discloses a lust for this hero of the glaciers so unquenchable that unless Daniel reciprocates instantly his denimed thighs will be drenched by a mini waterfall . . .

– So sorry, Danny. I was actually checking over to myself just how many cards I've already posted.

Why tease this Frenchman? I'll not see him again. No doubt he asks much the same of all tourists he meets on the boat, as they sit sharing a last pot of tea before bedtime. He's right. It would be commonsense to send a second round of cards from Srinagar. Danny's warning should not be laughed off. A fallible gay tourist could disappear, lured – for example – by that slim boatman who'll be mooring below us within minutes. Say I decided to give Danny the slip after supper and made off under the stars with the said boatman? Say further that I failed to show at breakfast? Whatever's happened to Mr Prote? Just what story would a flustered Second Secretary from the High Commission construct for London (having peeked under some remote lotus bed to inspect what roach and minnows had rejected)?

Another script for oblivion occurs to me as Daniel cleans his pipe.

Next week – tomorrow even – I join a group making for Zanskar. My pretended lust for adventure masks the hots for some first-time trekker with hair stolen from a Californian hive. Need I note his complexion rivals a king-size portion of peaches and cream? A tee-shirt? Well, naturally . . . and stencilled with a simple text. *They Call Me Golden Gate – I Open Up: You Sail Right In*. He's agile too, is young honey buns. I – years older and with chest thumping, not to mention throat harsh as a dry valley – bound to join him. I fail to clear the chasm. Had vanity not prevented Mr Prote wearing his glasses (the obituary begins), and had the shale not been treacherously loose . . .

– Don't think I need send more than another couple of cards, Danny. The neighbours who are watering my garden. An assistant who stamps my library books. Maybe a third . . . something special with black edges. I've a friend who's marrying this weekend. Sucked into suburban respectability at last. That really is the lot . . .

– I see.

Does he? The crumbs have been swallowed and the bulbuls have flown to try their chances on another boat. Daniel sucking some last particles of biscuit from his thumb is looking at me. I know that without checking. He knows I have refused his bait. If he also guesses there's no name at all scrawled under my heart at present, let him do so. I shall be spared any tiresome commiseration on a lonely existence. It might be amusing now to take the offensive and chase Danny boy back to his own half of the pitch.

– And you? Who's waiting in your chic but comfortable apartment back on the Ile, or is it Montparnasse? Who learns Danny's letters by heart and waits for him to share the duvet when Zanskar becomes impenetrable in November?

– Don't you remember I posted a letter on Boulevard Road this morning? That was to my wife. It could be almost a month before she reads it even a first time. She is in Sicily until October with a voluntary organisation.

– In Sicily?

– Well it is always possible she may arrive here before the end of the season. Tonight even. Oh yes. She has done it before.

My reticence vindicated in two matter-of-fact answers. Just as well I made no eager misreading of Daniel's picnic invitation. Now, had his easy manner and small gestures of intimacy been misconstrued as green lights, what observation or which movement on my part would have changed the signals to flashing red?

The put-down would have been gentle. He is very much at ease with English idioms. How would he begin? . . . My dear friend, you surely know the world well enough not to imagine every hand that rests on your naked shoulder (as yours does this instant Danny to lever yourself up) is anything other than a tiny sign that one human being is happy in another's company? Surely Ian, you cannot be yet another of those emotional cripples for which your country is so famous? You have travelled. You must have noticed half the world saunters with one arm round the shoulders of a friend. Who would adduce from such evidence that soon their arms and legs and lips will intertwine? Only those who are too much alone, Ian. Precisely what I suspect of you.

And so I make no direct comment on Daniel's revelation. An ironic smile conveys that I have noted his second glance at a newcomer. A white woman trailing behind her Kashmiri lover to within a couple of metres of our umbrella. Harem trousers of fine silk conceal what I infer from her stompy walk to be chubby legs. A chiffon veil clings limply to either side of her pale freckled face. The local lads discuss her with eyebrows and silent grins. They will think of her as the English girl. Tourism has not extended the language here. In Hindi she, Daniel and I remain The English that we were in colonial days. The young woman curls herself about the base of the next umbrella while her lover chats to his mates. I mutter to Daniel that liberation seems to be moving more than a little slowly up this way. He nods before buying us more apple juice from the portable ice-box strung round a waiter's neck. Having taken a first swig, he lowers himself again to the deck and sits cross-legged facing me.

– Charlotte and I are very different from those two.

– You amaze me . . .

– We have a very open marriage, you know. When we meet we tell each other everything.

– Everything?

– Indeed. I very much hope, Ian, that it is a way of life we shall continue for many years yet. Charlotte knows she is free each summer when I come to India. Before we went to the Town Hall to be married we had long discussions about freedom and loyalty, you know. Perhaps it is the same in England now?

Who leads for freedom and who for loyalty in these long discussions? The white woman twitching her veil to ward off flies would surely find such a situation unimaginable. But Charlotte? Does she accept Daniel's infidelities? Supposing he is planning to share tonight with the blonde swimmer who has the delicacy of a Dresden Shepherdess? Will Charlotte dismiss it as the small price of a shared fire throughout the winter? Would it be patronising to wonder whether she attempts to dilute Daniel's guilt by admitting to occasional fabricated affairs of her own?

– Well, I'd agree that there's a trend in favour of toleration. More people opt against old–style monogamy – or parodies of it. As you'd expect, it frets the traditionalists. Not the sort of thing to be encouraged among the workers . . .

– You are saying that open relationships are more difficult for ordinary people?

– Very much so. One example. Our dusty laws on homosexuality were liberalised some years ago. Now there are some of us who wonder whether those who changed those laws even considered the needs of factory lads. They were making England more tolerable for the undergraduates. Even using the word undergraduates rather than students emphasises a social divisiveness . . . but that's a digression. Sorry. I should be asking what Charlotte's doing in Sicily.

– This summer she is helping to run a centre for deprived children.

– Why not in India with you? Sufficient deprivation in Delhi alone, I'd have thought, to keep her on a twenty-four hour shift.

– But Ian, I explained it to you. We go our separate ways each summer. When I meet Charlotte she will tell me more about the Palermo project and about the American paediatrician she is sleeping with. She has sent me photographs of him. I have one of them together. That is to convince you that he does exist, otherwise you might think my wife and I play teasing games.

How very antiseptic and cleansing. Mutual confessions over the Christmas goose and oysters. Though the need to confess continues, you my Lord Cardinal are behind the times. Junk all those pokey boxes and the moth-eaten velour. Could I interest Your Eminence in our latest model? Note the stripped pine walls with just the odd rubber plant tastefully situated. Yes, that bedspread of white lace on which Daniel and Charlotte lie was run up from a couple of your spare surplices. No curtains here, you'll note, but these Parisian casements do open on a full moon discussing penetration with the Eiffel Tower.

– No jealousy hangups then? In either of you?

– Why should there be? Charlotte and I have shared secrets since our primary school days.

– The childhood sweethearts, eh? A village Romeo and Juliet . . .

– But our relationship will not end in tragedy . . .

– Presumably because your wife doesn't object to the odd one-night stand . . . with, say, that blonde on the next boat? I've decided to call her the Dresden Shepherdess, incidentally.

– I like that. Well, Charlotte knows I would prefer that to masturbation.

– That's very accommodating. You wouldn't regard it as a put-down of women? Only a mild one of course . . .

– But Ian, I was joking . . .

– I'm easily fooled Danny.

– The joke was against you, not against women. A test to discover how English you might be about sex. And you are. None of you can laugh about it. We say that is why you write the best pornography.

– Point to you. I'd not thought of that . . .

– As for the Dresden Shepherdess . . . all I have been asking is how I might relate to her intellectually. What about you?

– Isn't that rather what I implied?

If not later today, than certainly before Daniel strides off with his sherpas and his cocoa mugs I shall tell him that he invited a gay man out. It'll do him no good to pretend he does not understand the term. We'll have no *Comment?* no Parisian *Quoi?* about it. The French is *gai*, so nothing's ambiguous in the translation.

Daniel's face as he smiles at me is not unpleasing.

– And I do not think you are as alone as you pretend, Ian. Some people in London would miss you if you didn't return.

– There are one or two people without whom I'd feel diminished in many ways. Now whether that's reciprocated, I can't be sure. And that, my friend, is about as much as you're going to get on the score sheet, so don't probe any further about love or relationships or whatever . . .

We both laugh.

If he registers the absence of pronouns in what I've said he doesn't betray it and I don't care.

Without using my left hand as a lever I heave myself into a kneeling position – something I can't recall doing since I was thirty-five or maybe thirty-six. My right fist taps Daniel's chest and I wonder if he realises I'm sending up the hackneyed buddy gesture of American cowboy stars. I invite him for a quick dip before we change.

We begin our descent to the water side by side. Despite my warning to the two women I skid on some slime and shoot arse first into twenty metres of tepid lake. My invitation to race there and back using the nearest boat as halfway point is lost in a mouthful of water plus whatever top-up there may be of bugs and faeces. As I rebreak the surface and twist to face Daniel, I see him point towards me and shout with laughter.

– So who will be catching polio if he is not careful?

– So who had his sugar lump in London a week ago? Come on in . . .

Swimming at such any altitude is taxing and I must give in if the pounding in my chest becomes too persistant. Would there be any pleasure in swimming somewhere higher still? Would sex – incidentally – be any fun in, say, Ladakh? One must admit it could be a salutary taste of love life at eighty.

I chop across the waters of Dal Lake, changing from breast-stroke to crawl as I challenge a younger man fit from regular forays above the snow-line. The situation is doubly laughable. I hope that Daniel – twice the length of my body behind me – also appreciates the joke. Having frittered half an afternoon knocking macho games and gamesmanship, it is I who suggested he should pit himself against me. He cannot be expected to savour my more private joke against myself. Yet again, overcompensation rears its sniggering head as I – a gay man – strive to outdo the straight. A stupidity that may well prove my undoing.

The little patronising sod is giving me the lead deliberately. I swear it. He just has to have the resources to overtake me now as we avoid a weed bed and head for the landing-steps. Leading by one full length – my whole chest transformed to a thudding pneumatic drill – I grab at the guide rope. Daniel has gripped my left ankle and is shouting. I can understand his words despite the gongs resounding in my ears.

– Excellent Ian. You could tackle any of the passes in Ladakh. No trouble. No problem at all.

I tell him to piss off, having heard more than sufficient of all that. As I shake myself from his grip by stubbing my heel into his nose, I point to our boatman. A paddle is being waved in the air to attract us.

We are both combing our hair in the same spotty mirror. Daniel

– still naked – looks over my shoulder. After I have removed half a dozen brown hairs and one grey from my comb I straighten up. Daniel must have eased a pace to the right while my concentration was elsewhere. In the mirror I note his nakedness. Although he continues to push his curls into casual disarray I wonder if he wants me to be aware of his body. Is this perhaps a show he puts on daily for his trekkers? His nipples are two pink trouser buttons. Do heterosexual men go in for nipple play? That is, do they enjoy their nipples being gently teased? Probably not.

I lean to the mirror again to squeeze a pimple. In one downward glance I record that his pubic hair is gingerbread brown and his genitals are tiny but compact. I recall this impression when I move nearer the changing-room door to dry between my toes. Would it be unkind to ask Daniel sometime if straight men fret sleeplessly about penis envy? It would be and they probably do.

– One thing interests me Danny . . .

– Uh . . ?

– You're a city lad like me. How did you get into this whole Himalayan scene? I mean . . . all very understandable if you'd been reared in, say, Annecy or Strasbourg. Why this hunger for raw adventure in a Parisian?

He stands at ease pissing into a stinking galvanised bucket as I put my question. His thighs and calves have the tapering strength of the sprinter. There's a perceptible pause before he answers. Unfortunately he doesn't turn so I can glean little from his hesitation.

– I will tell you later. In the boat or maybe this evening.

The contrast between Bashir and the other boatmen fascinates me. His face to begin with. Always the face first. His skin – there's pleasure in reminding myself – is polished walnut shells among the heavier teak of other boatmen who are wheedling fares. Bashir didn't wheedle. That is why we hired him. His hair? As we glide into the weakening sunset, I compare it with a mess of thick copper wire. His grey eyes study me from behind Daniel's head. I leaned too long on the wooden balustrade while we waited for Daniel to dress. We already.

Possibly this twenty-year-old – twenty-two at most – isn't pure Kashmiri. His rounder features could derive from some young civil service sahib holidaying here two or maybe three generations back. Bashir – younger than either of his passengers – eyes the back of Daniel's head and then my face with a wordly frankness. For him the conscious need to bargain and survive began at the moment of birth. And that was probably here – at my feet – on the dry sacking of the family shikara. Looking at him, I find my earlier condemnation of the local men already being tempered.

There is a complicity in the looks we exchange. A silent dialogue of preplanning and speculation. Though I am sure Bashir believes I preceded Daniel from the changing-room deliberately (and it so happens I did not), little can be done to put him right on that. It is of no importance that Daniel sits between us. What does it matter that I can only offer the occasional unintercepted smile? Both Bashir and I know where we shall be tomorrow morning. Let Daniel scrape what acquaintance he can with the Shepherdess. If she agrees. I'll settle for a private picnic with this boatman.

– Boat now?

I decline. Daniel can hardly be left stranded in the middle of Dal Lake while searching the changing-room a second time for his lighter. Using the forefinger of my right hand I tap each finger tip of my left in turn. Finally I touch my wrist, where like most folk I wear a watch. The boatman nods. Five minutes.

Our second assessment of one another begins. I reflect on what I can offer him or he me – other than a sweaty fumble. This young Kashmiri, born a generation after his country's independence, is not handsome enough to be sought after with rupees and presents. If he were so, I'd not be among the bidders. Such bartering is open and widespread here. Propositioning on street corners seems to be more favoured than protracted restaurant courtship. Is it nothing more than the laughable whim of a holidaymaker that makes me wish he might see me as a person, rather than as another passing box-wallah with a supply of, say, shirts or cameras or dollars in return for the freedom of his body?

He puffs between calloused fingers at the cigarette he waits to be offered. His catch is graceful and the soft acknowledgement sounds to me like Tank you. Just how can I convey to him – other than by looking frankly into his eyes – that I've minimal interest in the shape or curving of his arse? It's a recordable fact at least that he hasn't crudely propositioned me by patting his crotch. Any tourist who strolls alone on Boulevard Road, whatever the hour, runs a wretched gauntlet of stroked genitals from hopeful beefcake boys.

He waggles the cigarette to refocus my attention.

− Boat tomorrow . . . yes?

Acceptance could edge on us into a tiresome routine. Daniel and I might be adopted as special passengers. I wouldn't wish that to happen. This afternoon has been pleasant but − in plain market terms − further time shared with Daniel would be an unprofitable investment. Unlike time shared with this boatman.

As my holiday whittles away, the appetite for a shared bed is returning. I consider the practicalities of smuggling a stranger along the warped gangplank that leads to my cabin. This boatman for example. Tonight. Would Daniel − chattering to the fair-haired swimmer − be too absorbed to note a Kashmiri skim in his shikara across the shadows around our verandah? And say he did notice? What's my life to him? On one matter I'm adamant. No joint further bookings of boats or boatmen with Daniel who − like as not − will be away tomorrow to Ladakh.

− No boat tomorrow. Thank you. No.

He shakes his head at me forcefully, yet the hair remains tight against his skull as if sculpted. Like our houseboat staff no doubt he dives night and morning into the lake. Those curls would be sticky to the touch. Suppose I were to arrange to leave the gauze window of my room unlatched? This boatman would not expect a one-night stand. Our friendship would need to be continuous and exclusive, ending only as I leave for the airport. All very pleasant too . . . Yet suppose again that this or any other evening I meet someone whose conversation is not limited to monosyllables and mime? How then could anything begun with this boatman be discontinued without bruising him?

− Boat yes. Boat tomorrow. Yes. Yes. Yes.

His tone is insistent. Almost shrill. He augments each syllable by prodding his thumb first against his own chest then towards me. If I were too stupid to perceive what he's implying, he ensures my comprehension by fanning a hand dismissively towards the changing-room from which Daniel must trot any second. I shrug my shoulders but then lean over the boatrail to smile down. I itemise my conditions with extended fingers like some stall-holder.

− OK. Boat tomorrow. BUT . . . One: No carpet factories. Two: No woodcarvings made by father. Three: No hash very special price from brother. Four: No shirts very cheap and hand-stitched by mother. OK? One carpet factory − just one − then you and me finish. Yes?

He claps his hands and laughs. He understands and is amused, I imagine, by the firmness with which I have presented my case. He flips his cigarette butt over the water, then rests his paddle and throws his arms wide.

– *Carpets? Go way. Shirts? No Tank You. You . . . yes. Me . . . yes. Tomorrow. OK.*

The conditions agreed, he lifts his left wrist and appears to be listening to his pulse while watching me. A moment later he shakes his wrist and inspects it with a frown. Finally he sits upright and begins to count his finger tips. I raise both hands with thumbs and fingers spread. He returns my signal with hands more slender than my own. Message understood.

We are both smiling as I tap my shirt pocket and say my name three times. He claps his palm flat against where his heart may be and replies *Bashir.*

Given a start soon after breakfast, we shall be able to share a whole day. The iron rations doled out by our houseboat kitchens can be supplemented with less soggy fruit and cake from the floating shops. We might swim together. Bashir can choose somewhere away from the favoured islands where affluent globe-trotters loll, supposing themselves to be children of the Heaven-born sahibs of yesterday. There must be dozens of quiet lakes and backwaters known only to locals where we can bathe and picnic and lie close under the high green umbrellas of the willow trees.

– *Tomorrow. OK?*

Daniel, sprinting barefoot with his lighter, joins us and hears only my last word. He touches my shoulder in assent, imagining I have been addressing him. I envy him his easy gestures. Not that my reticence in touching others stems from that dark fear which inhibits the sexually confused. Childhood lingers with me. More precisely early adolescence. A household in which affection was offered directly only to the family pets. Nothing between my stepfather and my mother. My mother withered to reticence by my father's death. Miles, a year older than I and more knowing from two terms at boarding-school, watches. Like an unsleeping guard-dog, he snuffles the air for any flurries of affection.

Even now, I seldom touch lovers in public spaces. Cautious in empty railway trains. Never in a market place. In my own walled garden a hug or cuddle is rarely initiated by me. Is it too late now to convert my brusque teasing of friends to the unpremeditated resting of a hand along a bared forearm?

The shikara is pulling us easily away. We swing out through weed-free water and make for the southern limit of the lake. The woman with cropped hair has dipped her sunglasses. It occurs to me that she and/or her friend might well have been watching the mime Bashir and I have just enacted. Certainly the Dresden Shepherdess is also following our departure. Are these women lightheartedly constructing a fable in which we three males feature? What I – for example – might be to Daniel? He to Bashir? Or Bashir to both visiting Europeans?

I wave to the women. After a tiny hesitation crop-head twinkles her fingers in response. Having observed the interchange, Daniel concentrates his interest immediately. The larger-than-life grin he turns on both women must appear even at such a distance to be some toothpaste commercial for the half-witted.

Not until we have rounded the prow of our swimming-boat does he look back at me.

– So. We now discover that you do know the two women. I should not have stayed behind in the changing-room, eh?

– Don't be preposterous . . .

– Of course you are going to explain that the waves you exchanged are only relics of colonial behaviour. Any white person always acknowledges another who is also toiling under the imperial burden. Another white that is . . .

My mother edges buttonholes with a skein of lavender silk in our tiny conservatory. Another smock. She is stouter by the week and will be like an elephant by my birthday. I trundle Rufus my wooden horse across the terracotta flagstones as she recalls for a visiting aunt one morning after the monsoon. On the jetty at Howrah she was joined by the Marchioness who said Good Morning. The former milliner curtseyed to the Vicereine, yet both at the time (my mother snips the silk with assurance) enjoyed an equality which seemed as permanent as the flies.

– Gandhi? Oh well, my dear, he was just a funny little creature in a dirty dhoti. Loincloth dear. He was nothing more than the subject of smutty jokes among the jute-wallahs just out from Aberdeen. Naturally I always pretended I didn't understand and nibbled away at my mango water-ice beside the tennis courts.

– Balls Daniel. And you know it. France had imperialists as well. No. No. It's far too hot to do a rerun of the Algerian war. Anyway, I'm not here to expiate the wrongs of my forefathers generations back. If we tread that road both of us could start to hate Italians because of the Roman occupation.

– I wasn't asking about your view of colonialism, Ian.

– Sorry. Well, I haven't a clue who they might be. Except that like me they are presumably holiday makers. Seriously though – when I was younger than you – I scootered through France and every British-registered car tooted.

– Whoever was on your pillion might have been attractive. And no doubt you were too . . .

– Don't fish. And for fuck's sake stop playing the stage Frenchman. If you don't I'll set you up with some randy grandma tonight and then tell everyone on the boat that Oedipus is alive and well and living outside French fiction. What say we have a drink with crop-head and the Shepherdess before you leave? We're bound to see them around.

– If they will agree I would be delighted. I still suspect they may be a pair. A long-term affair. Tell me . . . do you enjoy long-term relationships Ian?

A French summer in which, say, ten-year-old Daniel flew his kite over the Luxembourg Gardens. Mark and I lie seven hundred kilometres south-east of Paris. His idle hand forages beyond our tent flap until it closes on fat purple grapes. The bunch snapped off, he washes it in the lake. Water drips over our necks as he offers breakfast. Two fine years have begun. Almost two years to that flawless morning, one pitiful row. Nothing the same thereafter. All trust fragmented. Mark yelling:

– Do you want a sodding divorce? You were away. I was lonely and got pissed. He meant sod-all. Isn't loyalty better than fidelity?

We split. Another full year's silence before we meet for a beer. Mark's three months married, yet he fears he's paid too high a premium for respectability. Remembering occasions we have shared that lie beyond the golf course, the washing-machine and Sunday with the in-laws, he confesses to the sensation of having maimed himself. I tell him gently I'm not into furtive weekends (family commitments permitting) and leave my second beer untasted.

– Long-term? Oh, there have been one or two. Could be again but I'm not into advertising at the moment . . . Anyway – Daniel, do stop me if I begin another sentence with Anyway – meantime you were going to tell me about the beginning of your long-term relationship with mountains. If you talk fast and to the point . . .

– Something which you seldom do . . .

– OK. Point taken. I was about to say you could tell all before we touch the jetty.

– Not at the moment, Ian. My mind is already on my next

trek. Perhaps the sherpas have arrived while we were swimming. There is some equipment to be checked over with them. If you would like it we could still have supper together. I could tell you then . . . if you are sure you would not be bored.

– Not at all. We can't end the day with you still an enigma.

– I like that. Enigma. I find something enigma about you too, Ian . . .

– Enigmatic. Do you now?

– Perhaps we should spend a whole week together. You are so very good for my English.

But not so good for my well-being. Not one chance of a week, Danny boy. My days are slipping away too rapidly to fritter them on developing a relationship that offers no more than a distraction from, say, Bashir. Go your way, my clean-cut sportsman, and I'll go mine with this young Kashmiri at whom I not so accidentally smile. How else can I acknowledge the five fingers he is extending behind Daniel's fluffy curls?

– And had you considered I might not be so good for your concept of friendship?

– That sounds even more enigmatic, Ian. What . . ?

– No. Not now. Tell you more tonight.

We are passing terrace after terrace of houseboats. The Princess of Vales (Alexandra of Denmark? May Teck? Freshly repainted for our Di or merely a misspelling of Veils as in Salomé?) rocks placidly beside the Pride of Free Erin and divided from it by an insignificant backwater. On Sunset Boulevard tea and biscuits are being served beneath awnings to a macro family of Japanese.

Our own shikara slows and tips the landing-stage. Before we've even steadied, far less tied up, Daniel has clamped one foot to the worn pine boards. He is, I've no doubt, scanning the verandah for evidence of the anticipated sherpas or the equipment and stores he is expecting them to bring. Without glancing, he's already handed a two-rupee note to Bashir. This is accepted silently but the whispered confirmation of our private rendezvous is too enthusiastic for Daniel not to overhear.

– Ten . . .

– Ten? Nonsense. Two is all you're getting. We didn't arrive from New York this morning, you know.

Casually – so that Daniel might suppose it to be accidental – I drop my swimming towel across Bashir's bare walnut feet while scrambling from the boat. We both stoop to retrieve it. Our heads are so close I need no more than murmur:

– Ten. OK. Ten.

– Bashir. You. Finish. Him Go Way.

Our whispered confabulation seems pointless, for Daniel is pacing the deck to check catwalks on either side of the houseboat. No sherpas. No guests or staff either. He begins to scrutinise the boat next to our own which serves as an annexe when all other accommodation has been filled.

I too glance towards the adjoining verandah. Without thinking, I rest two fingers on Daniel's wrist, for I guess he is about to shout at one of the kitchen staff who is sleeping among the reeds. I jut my chin towards a chair-back indicating that a kingfisher is watching us. Although the gesture with my fingers was minimal, it was too full of menace for the bird. In one purposeful arc the kingfisher sweeps to the prow of a punt moored well out in the lake. I shrug and Daniel pats my shoulder.

– You are interested in all these birds, eh? These kingfishers and bulbuls? Maybe I should call you the English bulbul. Your hair is ruffled like their crests and you have bright eyes very like them too. By bright eyes I mean that you observe more than you pretend.

– So I'm a bulbul grateful for any leftovers I can pick up? You're a cheeky bugger, Danny . . .

We are wandering through the residents' lounge where the heat – trapped by window gauze and heavy awnings – has been pummelling the pannelled walls all afternoon. We are in a warm pine forest and the scent is stunning. Daniel leads on along the corridor that passes my own doorway. He stands in the door-frame of his room and listens as I twit him playfully.

– Now you may think I'm a bulbul. I'd say you were describing yourself. We all tend to do that, don't we? Unwittingly I mean. It's you who want to savour new experiences . . . remote monasteries . . . unmapped valleys . . . new attractive women. Now me . . . I'd say I'm more of a kingfisher, though rather less beautiful. I'm the one with the bright plumage who lurks by the water surveying what's on offer in silence.

He drops his head slightly on one side – if not like a bulbul, then what else? – as he considers what I have said. He unzips his jeans, but still does not reply. I'm aware that I too would be more comfortable in shorts, at least until sunset. When he has kicked his jeans back into his bedroom, he smiles at me. He has folded his arms and his feet are just slightly apart. I suppose him to be smiling because I've at last told him something of myself.

   – And when you have assessed what's on offer, Mr Kingfisher? What then?

   – The kingfisher tells no one which roach he has selected, Danny. He swoops. Then he's off with whatever has taken his fancy. If all the spectators gasp, he really doesn't give a shit whether it's shock or admiration they're expressing . . . So . . . what about a beer after supper? How about the Garden Bar along the road at the Maharajah?

My phrases are being picked over just as our sandwiches were a few hours back.

Daniel can make of my teasing just what he will. I notice his blackened hand again against the tan of his bicep. Would it be insensitive to enquire about that too over a second beer this evening? A childhood mishap in Paris? More feasibly some accident here in the Himalayas, when he was a less adept climber than no doubt he now is. I wonder whether Bashir might be a climber too. Like me probably he'd be inept once removed from his natural environment. For him the lake. For me the city streets.

As I light a cigarette and toss one to Daniel he is still watching me with his quizzical bulbul glance.

   – We make a strong pair, Ian. Not like those two women, of course. That is not what I mean. And naturally not in the way that Charlotte and I are a pair. But because we are in so many ways different, the one quality we have in common is a firm bond . . . I mean we both have daring. I take risks in the mountains because there I know exactly what I can and cannot do. I can sense a similar daring in you but I cannot isolate it yet. Maybe we should talk about these things later.

He seems to be in no hurry to move. I need to flop on my bed and write those postcards. Maybe doze for an hour before showering. Some rest from Danny, anyway.

My smile is open so that my firm move into the cabin doorway will not appear hurtfully dismissive.

   – Anything you like, Danny. But over that beer, eh? See you for supper.

And I close the curtain.

A BUS marked *Airport* trundles towards me from the Tourist Centre. Its progress along the crown of the road is so unpredictable that scooter taxis, together with vendors of soft drinks and fruit, scatter as it approaches. A tribe of sniffing mongrels also disperses. Rain that has refilled an archipelago of potholes in the tarmac sprays in the wake of the bus. Local schoolgirls already protecting their bleached saris with umbrellas and plastic capes dodge the muddy water more nimbly than I. One hop to the nearside of a treetrunk saves my jeans from a drenching, but I lose a third of the syrup just sold to me as coffee. A few extra stains across the only shoes I've brought with me to India.

Laughter from the open windows of this same passing bus infuriates me, until at second glance I recognise both Greg and Vince. They are blowing me kisses. Their flying outfits have been selected with some sense of style. Greg has a rainbow-striped balaclava tugged well down over his monstrous ears. I wonder if he is anticipating the need to protect himself from snow blindness even before take off for Ladakh. This could explain the jumbo-size dark glasses he's wearing, though maybe not those crossed owl's eyes that have been painted on the lenses. It seems a fair assumption that both actors are sharing one set of rainbow woollens. Vince has the matching scarf wound at least three times round his tiny neck and tucked over the tip of his astonishing nose. Greg wears the left hand glove and Vince the right. These they gyrate at me in sad but regal farewells. Vince dips his scarf a moment to yell that they'll see me in Leh.

– How the hell did you know I was going?

– Jean and Sally told us at breakfast. We called on you but you'd left already with glamour-boy. What's keeping you?

Details of the protracted haggle there's been over the price of a couple of new tyres seems unnecessary. My gesture towards one sherpa and the drivers squatting on the tarpaulin by our ten-ton truck serves as explanation. Vince glances and when he's conferred with Greg both close their eyes and clasp their hands in what I suppose is a pretence of prayer.

We may need that and more. The road by which we'll be setting out, presumably sometime before sundown, is still no more to me than the line Daniel has thickened on my map. Anecdotes related to me by returning travellers surface unbidden. Jean's packhorse for instance. One loose stone on a slippery shoulder and the wretched beast with half their provisions over the edge. Sally hysterical and unable to move for ten minutes. Much my own reaction, I suspect. At least with four good tyres and a spare, there's an even chance we'll negotiate the passes and arrive intact at Kargil. It would have been lunacy to have set out with the truck as hired. My reluctant agreement to be included in the party could still be called lunacy in retrospect.

Daniel is waiting. Jean and Sally swirl ice cubes in their glasses of campari and orange. They are silent and appear to be concentrating on nothing in particular. They too are waiting for me to speak. Daniel is becoming impatient.

The truck is booked for six in the morning. Both the drivers are very experienced. They will be on Boulevard Road opposite the boat.

Glances between Sally and Jean convey doubt about something that Daniel has stated as fact. Will the truck be there? Who has vouched for the experience of the drivers?

Daniel tugs his pipe from his jeans. As he repeats his offer, he looks away from us all to tap the bowl against his heel.

– So, Ian . . . Yes or No? The sherpas will travel in the back. You would be with the drivers and with me in the cabin.

To refuse would be churlish and illogical. The offer is generous. Why suppose that Daniel is merely interested in a couple more days conversation with me to improve his colloquial English? Far kinder to think he'll delight in showing a friend all the landmarks he has come to know so well these past . . . three summers? Or was it four?

Selfishly, too, it would be preferable to make the trip to Leh in the company of people eager to comment on the terrain. To share a truck with a personal guide and locals, who'll insist on stops where we can eat with their friends, just has to be one up on the jetsetting league. Who wants to be insulated from everything but comfort? To speed in a sanitised capsule between four-star hotels?

–You're on, Daniel. Why not? I'll be packed and on the verandah at

a quarter to six. That do?

He leans across to squeeze my shoulder while calling to the imp-faced waiter Ali for another round. Sally and Jean laugh. There is a resonance about the look that they exchange which makes me certain they had watched the arrangements I made with Bashir. I include both women with a smile as I comment artlessly that a trip through the backwaters of the lake I had been planning will have to be postponed. Sally stares towards the lake behind me as she wonders archly if I might not find something equally diverting in Ladakh.

— Not at all. I'm very happy with what Daniel's planning.

His face puckers a little as though detecting an undertow in the conversation. Jean evidently notices this too, for she distracts Daniel by pointing to rockets that are pluming across the roof of the hotel. Once he has turned she leans to whisper to me.

— Give me your boatman's name. We'll tell him you're away for a few days.

Lights at the intersection change. The airport bus revs so arthritically that Greg needs to cup both hands round his mouth as he shouts:

— Syllable by syllable rundown on your jouney, eh? See you in Leh. Nice to know you're off your bum at last. We thought you'd just sit and put the world to rights as the slime crept up on you . . .

Perhaps they hear what I yell as a reply. They must certainly note my annoyance as I bang my chest like a poor understudy for Tarzan.

— Not all fine intentions in here, mate. Not just whimsey-whamsey liberalism . . .

As the bus turns into Residency Road Vince shouts back. Sounds like Traaa. A convoy of single-decker buses follows them. Each one is destined from some day-trip tourist spot in the Vale of Kashmir. Along the bodywork of each crammed vehicle there's a bold claim in block letters that the bus is air-conditioned. Jean and Sally have already put me right on that dodge so it's not odd that every bus that passes has all windows pushed wide open.

When the last of the convoy has left I can see Daniel and Ting again. They sit opposite me on the far pavement. More accurately, we don't sit in the mud but on stacks of metal supply-boxes — old-style cabin trunks — that wait to be loaded. Daniel and Ting know each other well. They exchange presents across the continents at the turn of every year. Maybe as I watch them they are discussing Ting's children or Daniel's wife.

As I pour the residue of my coffee syrup into a puddle I giggle at the irony of these family men discussing their marriages. Each as they chatter away has his arm round his friend's shoulder. The fingers of their free hands twine and untwine, resting on the thigh of Daniel's jeans. Not one of the passers-by glances a second time. Few glance at all. And if I had a camera and snapped them now? In London I could produce a print with the casual observation that in some countries, anyway, men can demonstrate affection for their own sex unselfconsciously. And the response? A few smiles of disbelief, most probably, and no doubt the odd put-down such as *How charming to see gay love vaults so easily across both national and cultural boundaries.* Oh yes, I do still grudge Daniel his bubbling innocence. If proof is still needed that our British forebears have produced the weirdest crop of emotional cripples in Europe, then that proof's here, reflected in this puddle and the name's Ian Prote.

– You don't even need to tell us. You just have to be English . . .

Jean's own accent confirms my guess that they are from down-under. Now her opening words to me can't be based on, say, my stroll across the grass or my choice of shirt. Maybe I didn't stroll. We Anglo-Saxon males aren't strong on graceful movement. Even when looking for a loo we appear intent on locating a missing empire or a misplaced destiny.

Why should it have been anything but kindness that prompted Jean to beckon me to their table on the lower terrace? So I thought.

Ali with a Benares–ware brass tray hovers by me as I sit. The welcome on his face is the size of an elephant's cuddle. Both the women have paused and it's plain there'll be no further conversation until I've ordered.

– Gin?

– Sorry sir, no gin.

– You mean in Srinagar's only four-star there's no gin?

– Sorry. No gin. No spirits at all, sir.

The corridors and dining-rooms past which I've wandered on my way to these manicured lawns are cluttered with Americans and India's new Intermediate Class, as well as a rich assortment of Europeans and Australians. So what are they drinking, I wonder, as I try again.

– Chilled apple juice then?

Ali's smile withers to contrite possum. He mutters to his polished shoes what I take to be Dry Day. Certainly it can't be Friday.

Whatever the reason, there's not an apple fit for juicing in the Maharajah tonight. All very tiresome, for the humidity is still high despite a light breeze curling down from the hill-cleft and over the flower-beds. My choice is either to become irritated or give in gracefully. I wave at the two half-finished glasses on the table and suggest that Ali brings three more.

– Certainly sir. You also like campy oranges, sir?

Laughter all round. Prote blows it again. Ali gauges my reaction. Oh, but he does. The overtone in his question was unmistakeable. For once the international guide is accurate. Single travellers will discover that the Maharajah hotel has a cosmopolitan clientele. Decode that as bisexual, lesbian and gay. Add to it also those who are open to the odd adventure but not to classification.

Ali, then, is not slow on the questions. From his assessing glance, it might be fair to conclude he's no slouch in supplying most of the answers for solitary guests, either. It occurs to me that I might have to concede that Daniel is right. These two New Zealanders could be lesbian. Have they, like me, done little preplanning for their holiday other than checking out bars with (quote) sympathetic ambience (unquote)? A commonsense alternative might be that they've chosen this particular hotel on this Saturday evening for a good meal. Given just that, then it follows they might have agreed to end the evening among occasional gay faces that neither threaten nor bore them. Maybe like me they're irked by the endless after-supper anecdotes of bartering for tourist trash, that drift in a dozen accents across the houseboat verandahs until the teapots are empty.

We've scarcely exchanged the commonplaces that disclose I've never visited Wellington whereas they've visited London four times, than Jean is probing for details about my friend who was on the swimming-boat. Daniel – I explain – will be joining me – er-us – very shortly, but for the moment there's heavy negotiation down the road with a driver and his mate. I prattle on about the need for a co-driver who can scan the mountain stretches for blind curves, or shout instructions when the truck is moving very cautiously down the scarp of what Daniel refers to as the Dross Valley. Jean corrects me. It is the Drass River. Or did I say it t'other way round and was it she who insisted on Dross?

The rain is easing as I pull my map and guidebook from my shoulder-bag. The guidebook – appropriated by me late last night from a corner of the houseboat lounge – settles for River Drass. The locally printed map gives Dross Valley. Whichever is more popular – one can hardly say correct – our passports will be stamped there. While I'm in the middle of converting two hundred and thirty kilometres to English miles (*not* every six becomes a ten. Start again. Every ten diminishes to a six), I become aware that Daniel is standing over me.

– Everything is fixed. We can go. Ting will be back in a few minutes with some fruit. There will be no time now to stop for lunch if we are to reach the barrier at Sonnamarg by three. Here . . . by my thumb . . . Sonnamarg and then the pass. After three o'clock they would stop us. Every vehicle must be across the Koji-la before sundown.

– That's some comfort, anyway . . .

– But first, my friend, we must climb one thousand metres. Now if we had waited until January I could have taught you to ski, Ian . . .

– Daniel, I shall be deliriously happy with just a steady drive and two unbroken legs. From the views on these cards and from all I've heard, the journey itself will be quite enough for a townee like me.

And very probably more of a hike for my adrenalin than I'm anticipating. With any luck, there'll be no need for me to ask that we make an unscheduled stop when we're through the Koji-la so that I can calm my swirling guts.

Daniel doesn't anticipate any difficulty about my travelling with the group. This could be a very real possibility now that hitching is illegal along the Ladakh road. I've heard already from three sources the grim tale of an English girl, who three months ago slid from the rear of a supply truck and rolled through a gap where the road had subsided. One thousand metres to the rocks bordering the Indus headwaters. Daniel assures me the papers have been fixed. Ian Prote is now assistant guide to a group of French-speaking tourists through a territory of which he's no knowledge and a landscape dotted with temples or Buddhist gompas of which he knows less than nothing. As for geology or first aid . . . it is better not to think of either . . .

With the chirpy nod of a bulbul heading for nourishment, Daniel leads us to the truck.

We move through the drizzle into an older part of Srinagar and I try to guess where among the tangle of bazzars and busy squares the tomb of Yossa Asaf might be. Daniel admits he's heard the local story. Jesus of Nazarath, it's alleged, walked to Kashmir after that episode on Calvary. He married and there are direct descendants still around. We agree that a scrawled postcard to the folks at home relating how one had popped in to inspect Jesus' tomb before lunch might be quite a little show-stopper. When I'm back – not *if* I ever get back – from Leh, I must find a moment to locate the tomb.

Daniel, on the road he knows so well at last, is exuberantly informative. He explains rather unnecessarily that the houseboats we're passing are less gaudy than those designed for tourists. The contrast is obvious between the renovated Victorian extravaganzas that mark the tourist patch and these functional pine structures in which local families live. As we bump across a canal bridge that links Srinagar's twin lakes, I glance down. There are no expensive rugs on the cabin floors. No exotic stained-glass and gesso lanterns will be lit here this evening. It is reassuring however to be watching women stringing out the daily wash. They must be confident the weather will improve.

The relief driver, who sits beyond Daniel to my left, yells every couple of minutes to passers-by or shoppers who wait at intersections for us to pass. There's excited and good-humoured banter in Hindi, so I guess this must be his home quarter. The driver against whom I'm squeezed offers me a cigarette. He accepts my matches to light his own and pockets the box. My provisions for the journey are now reduced to five boxes of matches, plus one tin of lime and lemon drops purchased at Heathrow (and already half-empty).

Once clear of the outskirts, we all settle back. With one hundred kilometres to cover and no breakdowns we should – so Daniel calculates – make Kargil in roughly eight hours. This is going to be no dash along a motorway. I say as much to Daniel who shrugs as he opens an enormous pouch stuffed with documents and rupees. He concentrates on a list of the trekking groups he expects to meet tomorrow evening at some tongue–twisting speck on the map. By then we hope to be in the head-waters of the Indus. Not in them. By them.

The tarred road rises easily before us and the drizzle is turning to heavy rain again. By huddling down, I am able to peer through the windscreen during those moments when the wipers clear the view ahead. Fields flanking our route are still thick with the rich harvests of Kashmir, and along the simple main streets of villages through which we pass, hibiscus bushes have been shaped so that they spread as small trees heavy with purple blooms.

The windscreen-wipers squeak like a brace of unoiled metronomes. I'm aware that I've become less interested in the landscape than in following the arc traced by the wipers' blades. They affect me as a hypnotist's watch might do. They oscillate to a rhythm very like that of the song which Greg and Vince sang to us last night. But the words? These elude me, though I can readily recall keeping time with steady hand claps. Did the parody begin with Monday or Sunday? If I visualise Greg stomping towards our table from the balustrade while Vince thumped the waiter's brass tray. Of course . . . of course . . .

> *On Sunday you wish to search my anus*
> *Monday all our telephones are bugged I fear*
> *The Tuesday whatsit lacks . . . the something poofs and blacks*
> *Come Wednesday . . . what the hell was it? . . . Disappears.*

Has to be disappear.

– That music you're humming, Ian . . . it is the song that the actors were singing when I found you with Jean and Sally . . . yes? I heard it in Paris, I think, in an English film about war. The music but not the words. Vince and Greg changed them, perhaps?

– Right on, Danny. A First World War recruiting song. The original words that is. If the actors hadn't tampered with them it would all sound comfy and historic today.

– But the new words? I wasn't really listening because I was searching for you as they were singing. It did seem strange that at the end you all shouted *No! No! No!* instead of clapping. Surely actors want to be liked?

– Well those two aren't into traditional romantic theatre, Danny. I expect they'd say they're trying to jolt us all . . .

– Ah. Political theatre.

– What isn't? Anyway – there, I've said it again and you didn't correct me – they grab their audience by the shoulders and shake them so no one can flop back and dismiss what they're doing as a lovely performance. I imagine what they were trying to get across last night was the danger of something that's happening very stealthily in my country . . . yours . . . too many countries. That was what the song was about. I was hoping you might remember the words because I can't . . .

– Sorry I can't help. So what is it that's happening stealthily? That means like a thief in the darkness? Yes?

– Just that. See that raindrop plopping on the bonnet? There's another forming so unobtrusively we don't even notice . . .

– Yes. Yes . . . so what has this to do with . . .?

– Now think of a tap dripping steadily – stealthily if you like – on stone. Very slowly eroding it. The tap is the new rules and the almost innocuous little laws that are being inroduced to erode our choices and diminish all the options we've enjoyed. Vince was on the edge of the action, wasn't he? He banged the waiter's tray like a drum warning us that our liberties are being whittled down. Surely you must see all this in Paris during the winter when you've a chance to look around you and listen?

– Don't you think that there is some paranoia in everyone who is involved in political work, Ian? We have next to us in Paris . . .

– Hold it, Danny. Hold it. I have the words. Scribble them down as I sing, then you can translate them.

> On Sunday you wish to search my anus
> On Monday some phones are bugged I hear
> Our Tuesday High Street lacks all yids and poofs and blacks
> Come Wednesday newspapers disappear – two – three – AND
> On Thursday there's food only for machos
> On Friday night the road and airports close –
> By Saturday we're willing
> We'll even pay a shilling
> To trudge the road to Dachau
> The ash-grey road to Dachau
> And pop into a gas chamber for you–ooh–ooh

Daniel has not scribbled one syllable on the writing block that rests in his lap while I have been singing – off-key as usual – with my eyes closed.

– But Ian. It isn't like that. As I said, paranoia . . .

– Para nothing. It could become so. And soon unless people shout No! No! No! loud enough and quick enough.

– So where is your proof, Ian? Here we both are at liberty to travel . . .

– Sure, sure. For the moment. Can you swear that next year – alright in five years – there won't be some oil crisis or some great financial slump in West Europe? In two shakes of a yak's tail wages could become insufficient to take ordinary folk on a day trip to Calais. Throw in strict currency control and then, Daniel, you and I for starters won't be able to come and see for ourselves

. . . two more who must rely on what television cares to show them . . .

– Perhaps, Ian, you shouldn't be heading into the Himalayas. Maybe you should go home to London and build barricades like those in Paris I saw when I went to the *lycée* years ago.

– I'll be in London soon enough. All I'm saying is that Vince and Greg reminded me forcefully that I've allowed myself to become . . . complaisant? Yes, that's probably it. So here I am sorting myself out inside. You didn't write down the words, I see.

– Well, Dachau everybody knows. And I understand macho but . . .

Before he enquires – as I know he must – I explain yids and poofs. I add the rather gratuitous footnote that homosexuals are the last minority it is still safe to insult without fear of legal reprisals. Daniel hears me but I know he's not listening.

He wants to know if the term poof can be applied in English to homosexual women. I explain that in the actors' song it is a shorthand for both men and women. Attempting to deflect him from his obsessive interest in Sally and Jean, I ask whether he knows any gays or lesbians in Paris. He and Charlotte – or so he supposes – have never met any though they have watched and discussed television documentaries.

Should I impose on Daniel my distinction between homosexual and gay? One might begin by characterising homosexuals as the timid hordes less consumed with affection for their own sex than with a manic need to melt unnoticed into the woodwork of our society. Understandable, I could concede, in Moscow or Buenos Aires but surely not elsewhere. And gays? How to put it? Yes . . . gays are those who insist – as do Greg and Vince – on being visible and even asking for an equal handful of whatever crumbs democracy might have on offer. But should I then conclude I also ask for that, Daniel? Count me in, for I do too. Should I?

For I do. Yet it's as plain as the gradient on the tarmac before us that I've slid imperceptibly into a contentment that attributes decency and tolerance to all. My father's failing. Had he lived, he would have found reasons to excuse drunkenness in the oncoming driver. Two abrasive actors on route from Sydney to Aix and Edinburgh have spelled out my indictment.

So what is to be done? Should I scamper round London with banners and badges seeking publicity for this week's cause? I am too finicky. Too inhibited by the suspicion that I might be seeking to publicise myself. Even that is a crafty rationalisation I've concocted for my comfort. Yet say – next week or whenever – I nerve myself to seize upon some issue that occurs? Say I refuse complicity and will not keep silent? What will it achieve? Prote will join the unemployed, with time to contemplate his martyrdom over some small matter that fades daily like an unremembered headline.

None of this will do. Something . . . some course that is plainly sensible and within my meagre skills. A tiny beginning might be to point constantly at taps that drip everywhere, eroding what's been achieved even since my great-grandfather was a farm labourer. A small act of resistance to those who would obliterate yesterday . . .

– And you Ian? I don't think you heard me the first time. Do you know any homosexual women?

– Now Danny. Get this good and clear. Sally and Jean – I'm sure you're still brooding about them – were pulling your leg. They played a scene for you because they more than suspected it was the routine you wanted them to perform. It certainly deterred you from chasing Sally round the verandah last night at least. Whether that meant you had to masturbate until the crows started in the poplar trees, I and the rest of the world neither know nor care.

Daniel laughs and shrugs. As I pause to light a cigarette, I know he'll use the silence to counter what I've said.

– But you heard them at the Maharajah. Jean – yes? – the one the Shepherdess calls old sweepsbrush?

– Jean.

– Okay. It was Jean who told us about the double bed in Delhi. Now you were there to hear her, Ian . . .

– And I don't doubt it happened. They were simply selecting facts that would keep you guessing. You must admit they have done. Would you have been as fascinated if Jean with her boyish haircut had told you she drinks every evening at that garden bar because she's having it off with Ali the waiter?

– And is she?

– Oh Danny, come on . . .

– But it could all have been what you call in English a double bluff, I think. Do you remember the story Sally told us about the restaurant?

They're quite with-it here, you know. Not that either of us thinks it
does much for their own women. All these mediaeval arranged
marriages and what-have-you. Must say Jean and I have been given
very liberal treatment. D'you know back down at the Connaught
Grand Plaza in Delhi the night receptionist didn't flutter her lovely
eyelashes twice as she changed our reservation. She took one look at the
pair of us and popped us in a double so we could snuggle up . . . True
Jean?

– Every damn syllable. Tell Daniel about the restaurant. Ian won't
mind hearing it again, I'm sure.

– Well, we just don't know if the poor bloody waiter was suffering
from one of these eye defects you see everywhere round here. Maybe he
was myopic but vain. Plain fact is that when we went into Srinagar the
other night for tea . . . dinner . . . sorry, Daniel . . . the bloke insisted
on addressing Jean as Sahib throughout the whole darn meal . . .

– Oh that. Yes?

– She asked me whether I thought he was setting them up or
sending them up, I can't remember which . . .

– You nodded so she presumed you understood. Sending
them up. Making a joke at their expense. Exactly what both
women were doing to you if you had but realised it. They're
two high-spirited and well-travelled women, Daniel. Nothing
more. Tell me – is this the approach to the pass? The landscape
isn't as tame as it was half an hour ago.

– As tame? Ah yes. You should have brought a camera.

– I'll buy a few cards when we stop. Perhaps I might send a
numbered series home so I can be tracked . . .

– By a shepherdess?

– Do stop fishing or I'll stun you and reveal an unquenchable
lust for a shepherd who lives on an island in the Thames.

– It would at least be somebody.

– Well, I shall just put initials on the address so you can keep
guessing. Somebody – as you say – should know I'm heading
for the hills. I'll keep one addressed in my shoulder bag so I can
be indentified if we do happen to wobble over the edge.

– You must not joke about these things. After we have passed
Sonnamarg you will see a whole series of wayside shrines as we
move into the pass. These are not to the local gods. We do not
all jump down, Ian, and pray for a safe trip. These are memorials
to road workers and truck drivers. Some tourists as well who
failed to make it.

– You're not serious?

– Absolutely so.

Let me just be able to see that jeep three minutes in front of us as it pioneers the twists and turns along this scarp edge. A bus would be even more comforting. I could identify with the human cargo in a bus. Row behind row of tourists and pedlars, of maybe relatives as well, travelling in a group to some isolated village. That would be very homely. There might possibly be pilgrims too making for a festival such as my guidebook notes. A vast gathering each full moon in August among the stalagmites of a remote mountain cave. Even one distant bus conquering the thin rising line of the road ahead would prove to me that for many this route is merely an everyday trip. The settlements are smaller now and always more than twenty minutes apart.

I tire of peering into the rain on the lookout for an occasional straggle of sheep and begin instead to count the army trucks that are part of the afternoon's convoy making downhill towards Srinagar. They are a brisk reminder that we've entered territory in which the military have priority. I cross-check from a roadsign to the map on my knee and readily understand the military presence. We can't be further than fifteen minutes drive from the Pakistan border.

– So, how many times have you crossed the Koji-la Danny?

– Twenty . . . perhaps twenty-five times. I know it better than many parts of France.

– That makes me feel easier.

– Good. Then you can tell me why you so dislike the Englishman Miles, eh?

If I fold my map into its original creases very deliberately, Daniel may not notice my requickened unease. I can't know whether Miles is a regular visitor to India. Whether Daniel and he have met or talked. Of what interest can Miles be to Daniel? Possibly Daniel's interest in him is obsessive for some reason. Does what I can say of Miles provide Daniel with some key to myself?

– Since I arrived in Srinagar he seems to have been lurking on the edge of my life and I don't like that.

– Oh. You are imagining things. It may be a symptom of altitude sickness . . .

– Altitude fiddlesticks. He was behind the power-boat on the lake while we were picnicking. He was hanging around with his camera while Vince and Greg were performing. Wouldn't astound me if he turns up in Kargil ten minutes after we arrive.

– More paranoia, Ian?

– Balls. Alright. You might as well know. Miles is my stepbrother. No, I didn't know he would be here and there's no way he could – I *imagine* there's no way he could – know I was coming to Kashmir. We've not met for twenty years. I'd rather it was forty.

– His father is also . . .

– No. His father married my mother after my own father was killed. A car crash that also deprived me of a sister.

– I'm sorry . . . so you are not blood-related?

– Exactly. His father was a clergyman. A particularly fawning hypocrite trying to scramble up the social ladder. Miles, by the time he was sixteen, was proving a true heir. There are no more dangerous careerists in England, Danny, than the offspring of vicarages. I mistrust him and I'm wondering what he's up to here in India.

– But if he is a guide like me then he is just doing a job . . .

– Maybe. When he had the flawless profile of a Head Prefect his motives for doing anything were complex, take my word for it. Now he's coarsening round the jowls, I wouldn't suspect they've become less so . . .

Daniel accepts a lime and lemon pastille. The metallic lid of the tin as I replace it glints in the late afternoon shaft of watery sunlight.

A flash illuminates the lawns and the cabaret Vince and Greg are devising for us. It is more distracting than the lighting which throws the actors into relief among the shrubs. Miles is using his camera. Who is he photographing and what lies behind the self-obvious wish to record an unlikely performance on the margin of Dal Lake?

. . . I'll not be seeking Miles out for a drink if I find myself in his company. That's for sure.

– Are you trying to tell me Ian that you suspect Miles is more than just another Himalayan guide?

– I didn't say that. Am I taking his presence too personally, Danny? I don't really know or care what Miles Knightly does with his energy just so long as he leaves a cordon sanitaire between us . . .

– Interesting. That he may be more than a guide. I have wondered about this before. Sometimes there are holidaymakers here who . . .

– Oh we're into the espionage scenario now, are we? You, Danny, may not be who you think you've made me believe you are? Why not Jean and Sally using a lesbian cover, although they are paid by right-wing extremists in Wellington to pose as left-wing feminists? Do we chuck in Vince and Greg as well? Had we known last night what we know now we should have listened with extra care. Every joke concealed a White House secret and the number of syllables in every speech totalled the number of warheads in the Kremlin. Or was it Peking . . ?

Two actors bound towards us from a balustrade that borders the lake. One, tall as a guardsman, has monstrous ears and the face of a tired parsnip. It is the nose – shaped and tinted like a ripe plum – that I notice first as his companion comes trotting behind. He has to trot, for he cannot be more than half the height of the first.

We are not going to be able to ignore them. Having disrupted our conversation, they intend to compel our attention with their surrealist patter. Their knockabout routine has all the briskness of some inner-city pub show. For some not immediately accountable reason I feel they are not quite strangers to me. I have the sense of two figures erupting before me from a trapdoor during a dream.

Hello, hello, my comfy darlings!

> *Comfy might be an unfortunate word.*

True. Just don't finger your loo paper, lady . . .

> *Tends to set everyone's bowels off.*

I say, I say, I say . . . Can you tell me the airsteward's definition of happiness?

> *A dry fart at last when you've left Delhi behind.*

Cheeky slag. That's my bloody line.

> *You got that laugh last night. I'm entitled to equal laughs. Besides . . . I thought of it.*

Well you didn't get a laugh tonight, did you?

> *Oooh . . . maybe we've shocked 'em, duck. They may be genteel and*

like things in the proper order. Intro-
ductions, etc . . . Go on. You're the
extravert this week.

Well . . . good evening to you
liberal humanists everywhere. I'm
Pineapple Rita and je veux you
presenter my little mate Rose Sher-
bert . . .

Too kind. So what we gonna do for
'em tonight? What d'yer fancy as a
warm—up?

How 'about our tuppenny tour of
Jesus Christ's tomb . . . with com-
mentary?

You reckon this bunch wouldn't be
offended?

Let 'em stop us if they can. If you
think, our Rosie, I traipsed out there
in the noonday heat without gather-
ing usable material and tax-
deductible expenses . . . Say well,
will you?

Well?

You can piss off to the tit and bum
commercial theatre, me duck.

Always the pragmatic one was our
Reet. Mind you, I don't deny I
enjoyed our little outing. Some nice
sympathetic touches of local colour,
there was. All them carpenters' shops.
Lovely bit of lamb, too, in the but-
cher's on the corner. I always did go
for a well-dressed stage in the big
numbers.

That stone though, Rose. It wor-
ried me . . .

I could tell that. Some things need
not be articulated. I knew the thick-
ness of that stone they plonked on
him fretted you. You stood picking
the scabs on your lugholes. Reet's
worried, I mused . . .

51

*And with good cause. Like I said to
the custodian – I should hope they
found a heavier one than last time.
Suppose it happened again, Rosie?
A few as I could name'd get more
than Delhi belly if You Know Who
flicked it aside. Just say he dropped in
on some disarmament talks with a
bottle of home-made plonk and
enough fish sandwiches to feed all
India for a year.*

> *I do like a bit of pious hope now and
> again, Reet. Be realistic though.
> What'd yer reckon on that giant's
> footprint on that stone by the door?
> Genuine?*

*Nah . . . Early Henry Moore.
Has to be. Stands to reason. No
holes.*

> *Not hinting it never happened, are
> you? Not giving coded asides that the
> odd detail might be well-meant inter-
> polation, Reet?*

*Have you quite forgotten we're
booked to play Rome and Canterbury
this tour? Is there no end to your
speculative ad libs? Watch yer im-
agination and keep to the script.
Radical overtones without prior discussion I will not have. No wonder
Madam threw you out.*

> *Oh Reet! Reet – you promised you
> wouldn't. I only agreed to sing After
> The Bomb Was Over tonight if you
> didn't trash dear Madam Class
> Tones . . .*

*So that'll teach you to trust even
your dear ones. We live in the new
climate of suspicion. The script's
changed as of now. Rose, I've had to
amend it. Just vada this lot in front of
you. Sleek liberal humanists. Blo-*

ated with curried lobster and impecc-
able intentions. Get him there. You
could buy off any radicalism he's ever
had with a royal garden party and a
chocolate medal. Pongs of southern
England and the homo counties, he
does.

> Don't be cruel, Reet – you're hard on
> the well-intentioned when the mood
> takes you. Let him be . . . Take no
> notice, my treasure. You just keep
> making notes for Back Passage to
> India, if that's your thing. Ignore
> her.

We're waiting, you reluctantly
liberated hireling. Are you ready?

> Ready. Well now . . . If it hadn't
> been widdling down that Thursday
> just when I'd been to have me ends
> silvered, I'd not have sheltered in the
> Video Shop doorway . . .

Get on with it, will yer? You're
not starting a three-decker novel . . .

> You going to shut up or I? Right.
> I'm tempted by the title: Oliver
> Cromwell – The Naked Facts. If I
> hadn't succumbed I'd be with Madam
> still. Can't deny I enjoyed those
> years cooking and scrubbing for her.

Madam Class Tones. A professional with a purpose. None of yer
old world elocutionists. Madam is
fired with a social mission. Like
Hitler, you might say.

> There you go again, Reet. Bold
> brush-strokes as per usual. She will
> do it, folks – every issue reduced to
> Yes or No. No consideration for how
> the finer minds of our time are to earn
> a pittance.
> Madam has selflessly dedicated her
> life – I would remind you Reet – to

53

> eradicating coarse thoughts and sweaty vowels in all who aspire to public life . . .

Wouldn't rate me too high, would she, our Rosie?

> She'd not bother to give you a cold. Kill your reputation stone dead she would with a one-line dismissal. And smoothing the sateen revers of her evening jacket the while. A perfectionist through and through is Madam. I've known her slave the whole morning evaluating the sound of a vowel from three viewpoints . . .

While half the world's starving?

> Do I finish this? Do we have this ready for Edinburgh — Venice of the North?

My line, yer daft broomstick. Then you say: Don't you mean the Reyjavik of the South?

> If you say so. Think we should trim this a bit, Reet. Observe how restless they're becoming for our Dance Of The Seven Days to Dachau. Pavane coming up, folks . . . 'Tennyrate, I do concede Madam could appear arrogant to the uninformed.

Understandable. Doesn't she number among her antecedents on the distaff side a Laleham School Inspector? Isn't there a distant kinship with a Kensington church sidesman? Why be amazed that Madam should have imbibed the We Who Rule England complex with her mother's milk . . . Get on and interrupt me, yer daft faggot.

> I'd calm her with a simple lunch befitting her status. Ortolans au gratin of a Friday. The occasional flank of young artisan in April sauce. Her

                           demands became excessive, though
                             . . .

  What did her fancy run to then?
Sweetbreads of former radical on a
coronet of saffron rice?

                    Worse, Reet. Worse. Paraclete and
                    chips she orders. I bridled, Reet. Oh,
                    but I did. Madam you go too far, I
                    says. To dish up the Holy Ghost
                    with chips smacks mildly of elitism, I
                    demurs.

  So even you raised yer puny spine
at that. Sacked you, did she – there
and then?

                    Not till I added – this folks is where
                    the Cromwell bit comes in – I beseech
                    you Madam, consider that you may
                    be wrong. Out. Her mood was
                    imperative, I can tell you Reet. Out.
                    I'll not be questioned by the likes of
                    you, she goes. Scales fell from me
                    eyes . . .

  I'd have thought it would be tears
Rose – you being the last of the
grateful crumb-gobblers . . .

                    Scales Reet. I chucked out all me
                    evening class notes on Post-Nuclear
                    War Cooking Made Simple. I'm
                    liberated at last and not so much as a
                    drop of claret or a compromising
                    cheesy dip has passed these lips from
                    . . .

The noise of a jeep braking sharply distracts me and I lose one or
two phrases. I pick up on Vince again.

                    Reet . . . like you, I'm through with
                    non-commitment.

  Less of the casual innuendo. If you
wish to call me an activist, then do
so. Keep yer inferences to yerself.
This isn't the Civil Service.

I'm thirsty, Reet. Can't we get this lot to buy us a campy orange?

Aren't you forgetting something?

Alright then. Give that waiter a quick touch up so I can borrow his tray. Let's give 'em a hint of distant menace to close the show.

Sorry folks, we forgot the sheet with words on to roll down before your very eyes. Let's be hearing you nevertheless in our nightly showstopper Seven Days to Dachau.

On Sunday you wish to search my anus

On Monday some phones are bugged, I hear . . .

– Now you are sending me up, Ian.

– Am I Danny? Am I? You've set me wondering . . .

Poor bewildered Miles. The Head Prefect of yesteryear who missed the imperial fantasy by a generation. All his adolescent self-importance fragmented by collision with a world where personable looks and prowess on a games pitch are insufficient unless backed up by more family pull than a Suffragan Bishop can exert. So just what tatty secrets does he hug to his sagging pectorals as he struts the post–imperial highways? A marginal involvement with espionage might well nourish his underfed self-esteem.

– It is possible Miles is on some unimportant fringe of espionage.

– Working for?

– Who cares? All those buggers are ambivalent.

– Perhaps he suspects that one of us is also an agent?

– Aren't we all in a minimal way? I mean whatever we choose . . . whatever we dislike underlines something we believe. But Miles, I suspect, won't be on the lookout for agents so much as assessing other English people here for what he'd call reliability. Yes, that would suit him. The watchful prefect noting character defects to report to the headmaster.

– Smoking in the toilets?

– Well, smoking dope or carrying it. That would suit him. Sex, of course . . . if possible with children.

– But you, Ian, are in the clear naturally?

– I allege and attest I'm Ian Prote, born in London but at home in all cities and more or less at ease even in the Himalayas. A happy dissenter and a compulsive lover. Like my father I'm inclined to take strangers on trust until I see they're trying to double-cross me. So I assume you are who you say you are, though I'm not yet ready to swear you might not be collecting information about the convoy that has just passed, or this military post we are approaching . . .

– Come on, cynical Englishman. We're at Sonnamarg. It is necessary for us to get out for a moment. They will know our papers are in order but they must be stamped. I pass here every fifteen days . . . but as a guide with no interest in Indian politics . . .

– Makes life more comfortable but . . . Don't say Vince and Greg didn't warn you that the chances of things continuing that way are diminishing . . .

The village is little more than an elaborate military check-point. A damp string of cafes and tourist bazaars border the road on either side. It's not only the military police who wave a welcome. Travellers returning from Ladakh glance up from the postcards they are writing or from the soft drinks they're sucking through straws. The camaraderie of those passing in desolate places is evident for the first time. As Daniel waves unselfconsciously, I can't resist reminding him that only twenty-four hours previously he was twitting me for acknowledging Sally and Jean in just a casual way. He apologises and says he'll buy me supper in Kargil.

As we settle back in the cabin and light cigarettes Daniel nudges me.

– One more word on spies, Ian. You say you have travelled a lot. Have you ever been approached to collect information?

– Oh sure. Once or twice. I've always declined with the admission that I'm bad on team loyalty.

– So you have met agents?

Congo Katanga 1960. London journalists tell me at the bar that another lad arrived during the day. A photographer from Lusaka. That city of third-rate minds scuttling between unmemorable buildings, in one of which I taught. Lusaka, from which I've ducked out on holiday and found myself surrounded by a war. A city with three professional photographers. Correction . . . without Tim, only two.

57

The man at the window table is a stranger. He's uneasy meeting me and quite discomforted by my artless questions about Tim Frampton and Tim's kids. All in good shape he tells me. I reveal that Tim was hideously disabled in a crash six months back and was never married. I further suggest that the newcomer pisses off back across the border pronto to his Special Branch pals before the Fleet Street heavies suss him out.

Tim poised on the arm of my chair. Hair rich as fresh fallen chestnuts and a touch light as swan's down. Reading Marlowe to me, for Christ's sake, until at last I understood . . . Tim . . . two-timed by me. And for what? The constructed smile of an incurable gambler . . .

– One or two part-timers. The little people who need to look big to themselves in the bathroom mirror.

– Like Miles?

– As I said – who knows or cares? Just be aware of him. If you catch him sniffing your underwear shove him in the lake.

Daniel grunts. The heater is now on and the warmth in the cab is beginning to make him drowsy. No doubt he was up and busy checking stores and documents earlier than I was this morning. There are no sounds from the back of the truck. When we last checked through the shutter behind our head, both sherpas were sleeping with their heads resting on padded anoraks. I too would like to rest my eyes but am terrified this might set a trend. Both drivers appear very relaxed as we snake back and forward up into the Koji-la. There's some comfort in reminding myself that they use this route even more frequently than Daniel.

It is mildly amazing that I find myself less tense as the hours pass. There's a security in being perched here with five others and half a truck of equipment and stores. I can make myself believe we must be weighted heavily enough on the crushed rubble surface to survive anything but a head–on encounter at a blind bend. I no longer envy Vince and Greg the safety of the morning plane. By now they will be in Leh and most probably are concluding their first impromtu performance in the main street. What will the local traders make of them? From a photo in my guide book I gather market folk sit cross-legged on the kerbs, with mounds of radishes and potatoes spread before them ready to sell to those tourists who prefer to cook for themselves in hostels. Can the hotel food there be worse than the houseboat on Dal Lake? I begin to anticipate a good supper in Kargil – and at Daniel's expense. He's a generous man.

Daniel insists on buying drinks for Greg and Vince while apologising that he joined us too late for anything but the end of their show. The sharpness of Greg's response is blunted – but only a little – by his downcast glance.

– End? Beginning? You'll be wanting a middle next. The only end to shows like ours will be when the dafter machos in a bout of daring start aiming darts with nuclear tips at each other.

– But I was only trying . . .

– Just what we're doing too. Before time runs out. Twelve minutes after the first big bang they'll be running up white flags over the global rubble . . . and even that won't be the end.

– Sure enough. Big Greg and I will be capering around somewhere as the temperature slithers down to a Himalayan winter.

A somewhat bewildered Daniel protests he's merely a mountain guide. With well meant generosity he indicates I'm an innocent holidaymaker. Vince – confident that he has stirred us all with the cabaret and the epilogue – grins round the table. Greg toasts us in campari orange and looks at me while sniffing that there's little point in hiding from the world up a mountain. When I defend myself by explaining that I need somewhere to relax and sort myself out, Vince fishes an ice cube from his drink and – between crunching it – wonders why I can't do that somwhere in the Balls Pond Road. The only refutation open to me is to point out that in Kashmir I'm alone among people who do not speak my language (Bashir for instance) and whose culture jolts my apathy at every street corner. In the Balls Pond Road either the milkman calling for his money would distract me or I could funk out of solitude by calling a lover.

Jean suggests both actors might be prone to stereotypical thinking. To be white and in one of Kashmir's best hotels for a drink needn't imply the callous self concern of jetsetters. Sally supplements this by telling Greg he should check before concentrating on the converted. Both women, we learn, are involved in the New Zealand peace movement and have contacts among the Greenham activists.

– Okay folks. Just remember us as a reminder to you all and keep protesting.

Cigarettes are offered round as Daniel accepts a badge from Greg. He agrees to wear it in Paris. Smiles from everyone for two seconds or less. Daniel blows it by adding that he does still prefer theatre and films that tell a story from beginning to end. Vince explodes, spraying the turf at my feet with campari. Greg collapses with elaborate despair, then – getting himself together – shrieks at some ducks who are squawking beneath the balustrade.

– If it's a story you want, my ducky duck, go read a fucky fucking book.

The pitch of the engine is higher. The back of my neck aches from too long a rest against the worn unpadded leather behind me. I pull my head upright and notice our headlights are full on. When I look towards our driver he nods before shoving my cigarettes and matches along the dashboard ledge. He is already smoking one.

– Good sleep?

It must have been, though for how long I slept and how long I recalled last night at the Maharajah I've no notion. We have now climbed the pass and seem to be descending very cautiously. The driver exhales and shouts Drass over the roar of the engine, undulating one hand to the left like a playful dolphin. I guess he has to be referrring to the river somewhere below the onside window. There's no evidence of any settlements yet. The only light other than our own is from something heavy on the skyline lumbering towards us.

– Angry . . . angry . . .

We are edging round a curve, so by leaning forward in front of Daniel I can see what he means. Although we are still high in the head-waters, I can glimpse the river crashing and rearing against boulders that impede its course.

When I've settled back, I notice Daniel is slumping farther and farther down on his quarter of the bench. His head flops from side to side with increasing violence as the driver wrenches the wheel full lock to left and then right. Before Daniel does crack his skull on the dashboard, the co-driver and I exchange a glance and a grin and haul him upright by his hair. He shakes his head and blinks amiably at me.

– Thank you Ian. These trucks always make me drowsy, you know, after an hour or so. Would you mind very much if I sleep with my head on your shoulder?

What's to be said but OK? Daniel has demonstrated to me over and over in our brief friendship that not every physical brush should be construed as homoerotic if the toucher and the touched happen to be of the same sex. That his head lies easy on my collar bone is no guarantee he'll not keel forward to smash his face on the guard-rail. If this engages some fraction of my attention for the next hour or whatever, it's still no great price to pay for a free trip and a supper.

His proximity reminds me of Bashir and I hope either Jean or Sally or both will have seen him. Made him understand too that I wasn't fobbing him off with a promise I'd no intention of honouring. I need Bashir in a sense that Miles, for instance, would never understand. There'd be a chilly raising of one eyebrow as he asked how I, a democrat, enjoyed patronising the locals. Only Bashir can involve me with these landscapes and these people. Without him they will lie flat and garish as the postcards in my bag. Daniel, Jean, Sally . . . Greg and Vince all fine but all – like me – Caucasians in transit, wandering briefly across a harsh, unyielding surface. Jean and Sally perhaps construe my planned outing with Bashir as a light interlude. Vince and Greg might be more sympathetic to my halting explanation. Unlike Miles they're not inhibited by laughable barriers or fusty convention.

    – *Goodbyeee. Remember to keep shouting No! No! No! all you fat cats . . .*
    – *Remember Pineapple Rita and Rosie Sherbert, eh?*
    – *Shout No! now, because the choices are narrowing, folks . . .*
    – *If you don't dissent we might as well be fitted for our winding-sheets, don't you agree Rosie?*
    – *As always Reet. As always. I have heard as how the better type of asbestos winding-sheet is beyond the purchasing power of the likes of us . . .*

    They trot to the balustrade. I can't believe they've kept a boatman waiting throughout their performance. Only when we have all followed them to the wall do we discover they've hired a shikara and taught themselves to paddle it across the quiet lake.
    They glide in jerks away into the darkness. Greg's taller outline kneels at the prow. Vince straddles the stern. His stubby legs feather the water behind them. Sally wonders – quietly so that Daniel does not overhear – whether the two actors may be lovers. I guess they may be friends who love one another but do not make love.
    Of course they must be able to see us waving to them, outlined as we are by lights along the hotel verandahs. As a reply they offer us an astringent lullaby chanted hideously off key:

> *Pale hands I loved beside the Shalimar*
> *Where are you now? Of whose crotch do you smell?*
> *Pale glans I loved in youth hostels afar*
> *You snatched my cherry . . . may you . . . rot . . . in hell .   .*

The driver has changed from bottom gear now that we are moving along more gently graded stretches. Occasionally I distract him by indicating clusters of light, high above the road on either side. He mutters what at first I take to be the Hindi for village or perhaps farm. Even the noun for monastery, since we've entered Buddhist territory. Only when his response has been different a fourth time do I suspect he must be naming settlements. If it were possible to move without causing Daniel to bang himself on the bodywork, I'd be able to check places on my map and calculate how long remains before I can ease my legs and concentrate on supper. There's a perceptible jauntiness now about the way in which the driver is handling the truck. I hope this derives from his recognition of familiar landmarks – an outcrop or an overhanging tree which means no more to me than the last one or the next. He no doubt is getting hungry too.

At the next bend there's a stamp on the brake and we somehow avoid flattening a flock of goats being driven home late by a wide-eyed boy of maybe eleven or twelve. His head, like Bashir's, is round as a cannon ball but his fringed black hair drops forward on his brow in Tibetan or Chinese style. Somehow I register all this as I help the co-driver to steady Daniel.

Although the engine has stalled and is now being churlish about starting again, Daniel does not even sigh in his sleep. The co-driver frowns and looking first at me nods at Daniel. He's probably becoming bored with our task of saving the tourist guide from injury. We cannot be more than fifty kilometres from the small hotel in Kargil where Daniel and his team stay. It seems a fair assumption that with the road broadening out there'll be no more emergency stops. I grip the guard-rail with my right hand and close my eyes.

It is impossible to doze. Daniel has been slumped against me for so long that the circulation in my left shoulder and down my arm has been interrupted. There's little to be done but exploit my newfound policy of matiness. I extricate my tingling arm and insert it round his shoulders. As my hand flaps loosely, I sense the blood returning. If the co-driver would stop choking on the cigarettes he also filches from me whenever he supposes my attention to be elsewhere, I could sleep. After one more protracted bout of coughing I feel an inrush of freezing air and realise he's opened the window. I accept gracefully that I am just not going to be able to doze.

As I reopen my eyes I focus on Daniel's left hand. Like my own fist it is clasped round the guard-rail, except that my right hand is tightly clenched and his left hand is not. With every lurch of the truck his thumb edges nearer to my fist.

The midnight-thirty train to Plymouth carries sailors from weekend leave, plus Monday papers, plus me. I've no objection to the young rating who wishes to wedge the compartment door so that we can stretch full-length and sleep on the cushioned seats. Sure, it might be a good idea to remove the light bulbs and pull down the leather blinds.

Neither of us says goodnight. I lie on my back wondering how many more times I might see my mother alive. How welcome I might be then to visit my stepfather and the humourless Miles. Always supposing I've any wish to do so. It might be best to start shifting my possessions gradually.

The sailor from Nottingham clears his throat twice.

We are passing some suburban station and in the filtered light I notice his eyes are shut, but his hand has trailed onto the carpeted space between us. The fingers are spread slightly and his hand resembles a fluted cup waiting to be filled. I turn on my side. Now facing him, I drop a gentle fist no more than three train sways from his finger tips . . .

Steve. No inhibitions. No nervous breathlessness as he wedges himself back among the cushions and I uncurl against him.

– Steve's the name . . . Don't go too rough though, eh? The old appendix scar's only just healed up.

Our truck pulls sharply to the left. The full moon is sufficient to silhouette three small boulders in the middle of the tarmac. Daniel – who or may not be still sleeping – lies across my chest. His thumb continuously probes and prods the space between the warm brass and my curled fingers. I stare ahead as the truck is inched round to the far side of the boulders. Daniel's thumb begins to stroke the base of my index finger.

Hello . . . Can you hear me Gay Helpline? Listen. This is most urgent. I have a blond problem . . . Well, he's married and by daylight he's into women. It's dark right now and he's nuzzling into the vee of my open neck . . . What d'you mean, get on with it? . . . We have company and I'm trying to behave in a principled way. Is that all you can suggest? . . . Now just you listen. I'd no reason, nor the slightest wish to think him interested in me . . . I did not, I tell you. I did not think of him as a sex object. Cut the theory and listen. Just before the pips cast me adrift on the unknown I'd like you understand that he's beginning to rub his thighs steadily against my own and neither one of us is exactly fourteen any more . . . Do not be preposterous. Have him? I can't have him with two drivers watching . . . Well. If self-control is all you can offer as an alternative I might as well have spent my rupees calling the Prime Minister. All I'm saying is we'd just better see the lights of Kargil soon or we'll need to find a dry cleaner who can cope with two pairs of soiled jeans overnight . . . You want to what? . . . Well, you can log the call as *Bewildered – Western Himalayas – Asia*.

I consider whether Daniel may be some kind of prick-tease. Perhaps – and if so he has a bloody nerve – he sees in me an interesting alternative to masturbation. Does he imagine that he's going to steer us towards some mute infantile cuddle in some flea-bitten dormitory? Maybe – though I'm increasingly uncertain how effective a remedy it might be – maybe if I concentrate very, very ruthlessly on Bashir I might find Daniel's damp and sweaty hair less erotic as it strokes my lips.

– Kargil.

Our driver shouts the name. It is like a victory cheer at the end of some contest and he repeats it as he flings the engine into top gear. Although I shake his shoulder repeatedly there's no reaction from Daniel other than a grinding of his teeth. Question – is Daniel asleep or is he giving a very competent performance? I shake him once more and he turns a slightly smiling face up to my own.

The hell with both drivers. I kiss between the two furrows on his forehead before whispering to him for his private information.

– Kargil.

He frees himself and struggles upright, blinking at us all. It is a very professional performance. He rubs his face, then yawns and reaches for my cigarettes. Is it courtesy or intimacy that prompts him to light one for me also, before enquiring if he has been a nuisance by sleeping on my shoulder? This invitation to complicity annoys me. I counter by asking if he has been enjoying a pleasant dream about Charlotte or Sally for the past half-hour. The first street lights of Kargil aren't exactly Blackpool's Golden Mile, but they are bright enough to define the coldest look I've noticed on Daniel's face. Without answering, he throws the half-smoked cigarette through the cabin window and – leaning across me – directs our driver towards the overnight stop.

THE MENU is chalked on a wall in four languages. Pink scrawl on a limewash ground. Thick noodle soup with chop suey to follow. Not what I would have chosen after seven hours in a truck, but then I am not paying. Daniel at the serving-hatch cum reception-desk appears to be settling in advance for our meals and our bed spaces in the dormitory.

Daniel insists on picking up the tabs for all the campari oranges we have consumed. Greg and Vince have left theirs anyway and the New Zealanders' protest is vigorously overruled. Daniel explains he must leave us to place a call to Paris before his bureau shuts. It seems to me that both Jean and Sally are also ready to leave, but I order one final round when I return from seeing Daniel off from the jetty. As we wait for Ali to bring the drinks, Sally wonders whether I accompanied Daniel merely to confirm arrangements for the morning. Jean notices that I appear genuinely puzzled.

– I reckon she means, Ian, that you might have been giving all the boatmen the once-over on the offchance what's-his-name – Bashir? We must remember his bloody name, Sal – might just be waiting for you under the willows.

I shake my head, and do so again a moment later when Sally asks if whoever may be waiting back in London is happy to turn a Nelson eye on my odd holiday escapade. It is so much easier to chat more openly to these two women than to Daniel. I use the opportunity to make very clear that I'm not searching here or back at home-base for any long-lost other half.

Jean repeats what she and Sally must often have discussed. To her, romantic love's a drug and she's certain that she's long since cured herself of dependency. She's played what scene there is in Wellington and now – at thirty-five – has settled for a bloke to whom she found herself returning with surprising frequency after their first meeting seven years back. She admits to an easiness in his company that constitutes for her the only sense she ever has of being at home.

Sally – rather more like me – feels adequate in her own company. Again like me she's delighted when lovers ring and then arrive almost unanticipated for a long holiday weekend.

The camparis finished, both women make for the loo. I amble to the jetty to bargain with a boatman. Yes, I do peer round for Bashir, but he's probably sleeping in the battered punt that is his home. I consider giving Jean some rupees so that she can – in apologising for me – recompense Bashir for some of the day's fares he'll refuse in the morning. This would be a bad move for he might well feel insulted, and the women would smile wryly at a gesture that could only negate any arguments I might construct in favour of friendship. A movement by some azalias̄ to my left distracts me. Miles is moving away from Ali in the direction of his parked jeep. It's wildly improbable that those two have been making any personal assignation. So what then have they been discussing? There could just be a grain of substance hidden in that lighthearted conversation Danny and I . . .

– Along here, Ian. The sherpas will bring your bag. No, you must let Ting carry it, not because he is a servant but because you are a guest. You like Chinese dishes, I hope?

– Given some choice . . .

– Excellent. Our supper is ordered . . .

He drops his left arm round my shoulder as he guides us both along the earth-floored corridor with a candle stub.

– I must look after all your needs, Ian. Then you will go back to London and tell your friends that *chez* Danny it is *tout confort.* Yes?

OK Danny, my friend. OK. I've checked your code. Just do me no favours. I don't need you as much as I suspect the prospects of having me excites you. Ian Prote is not about to play understudy to your wank rag, old lad, just because you are temporarily deprived of fascinating women. Don't chuckle too nervously as you throw your luggage on that truckle bed adjacent to mine in the far corner. Let that exhausted driver or whoever he is snore as loudly through the night as he is now doing. There'll still be no sneaky after-lights-out groping games tonight. I'm tired. We'll play it cool and see what you can devise tomorrow – if there's any substratum of affection beneath your boyish lust.

– Surely, Danny . . . Look . . . I hope you've not ordered king sized portions of chow mein. Well, not for me. I really am half-asleep already.

– Not your stomach again?

– No. No. Just tired.

– You must eat something, though. I thought you might want to talk quietly later on. That is why I chose two corner beds for us.

– Very thoughtful of you. Can't we talk tomorrow?

– But of course, if you would prefer that . . . We shall not have very much time more together, shall we?

– There'll be tomorrow night, won't there? I'm sure we'll manage something.

– *Stop worring about Bashir, Ian. He's asleep long since. You'll have us all in the drink gawping at every shikara . . . Anyway – who knows what you might sumble into on the road to Leh?*

– *Sal's right. I'd say Danny boy wouldn't be adverse to a tumble in the wheat fields. Wouldn't you? All coy and blushing, mind, and loads of however did this happen . . .*

– *Shut up the pair of you. The man's woman-mad. No, come on. He is. Didn't I spend all the afternoon with him?*

That bulbul look again. Head quizzically held on one side. I try not to look into those blue eyes and push past him, suggesting that we go to eat.

Daniel has consumed today's lunch with as much gusto as last night's chow mein. There is an enthusiasm that informs everything he does and says now that he is here in the mountains at the very gateway of Zanskar. Before we'd hopped down from the truck onto this gaunt ledge of shale and baked sandstone, he'd grabbed the back of my head and pointed it south-east in the direction that he'll be leading his sherpas and trekkers. It crossed my mind, now as I sit on an oil drum in the sun, that he may suggest sometime today I should abandon the road to Leh and accompany them. I am after all accredited as an assistant guide.

If he does invite me I shall decline. A full day and a night in Daniel's company has been fun, but the need to experience Ladakh raw – not filtered by Daniel's comments and recollections – surges in me. I think of Bashir and wish he were here. Although he is younger than Daniel by years, his approach to any relationship that might develop between us is more mature by far. I review what I have just thought and wonder whether I'm too jaded, but then decide what I'm really rejecting is the obverse side to Daniel's boyish enthusiasms. Inevitably our silent courtship in the truck last night recalls the shy uncertainties of two adolescents. For me to pretend to revert to that is laughable. Not that I shall say No tonight, but he must make the running. Helping lame nervous virgins over stiles has never been my scene.

Daniel must choose. One of two rooms. The hunchbacked manager who has sold me smuggled half-price cigarettes offered us a twin-bed or a double. Our bags are stacked against the rest-house wall between the two door-frames. The very instant I began bargaining for cigarettes, Daniel loped away to the roadside. A pointless evasion, for he must choose. He chats in the midday glare with a multinational cluster of travellers as they wait for the military convoy to pass. When the road is clear, two or three buses will grind round the cliff face, no doubt towards the head of the pass. Tomorrow I shall be standing thereabouts while Daniel heads east with his trekkers, if they ever arrive.

Daniel must choose our room and in so doing make a statement. If all the cuddling against me, all the hand-holding with the sherpas, has been unconscious and just casual *bonhomie* – why then, let him lug our bags into the twin-bedded room. Should he however throw our things together on the double mattress, then he is not saying but shouting that he is eager for us to be even closer than in the truck. And on that double bed should he pretend to me or to himself that he's no inkling I am gay, then his self-deception is either more complex than I've encountered or he hasn't the perceptions of his own backpack.

My yell distracts him from a conversation with two very English-looking students. He waves both hands above his head in acknowledgement. I signal that I'm going for a shit and leaving the baggage to him. He answers with a thumbs-up and turns away. No doubt he's offering tips and information to the two young men in sweatshirts stamped with some college badge. The scarlet printing has run with constant washing and now blotches the white cotton, so that their clothing appears to be an extension of their scorched arms and legs.

The latrines are well beyond the dusty scrub and clumps of mountain flowers surrounding the rest-house, a little distance from the track that slopes into a dry valley rising again to wind away to the village. Only the tips of gompas set on high outcrops of sandstone are visible. The placing of these loos has not been haphazard. A clean prevailing breeze scoops up the nauseating stink from the earth holes and thrusts it across the slopes well above the village. There's much discussion among ecologically-minded tourists on the houseboat about the local tradition of using animal and human dung as fertilisers or even as fuel. A pity, I think – dragging open the corrugated iron sheet that serves as a door – that the practice hasn't been extended to this foul pit.

I visualise ruefully the privileged who speed through India in air-conditioned coaches. Evenings in cool hotels where selections from *My Fair Lady* and *West Side Story* are played by trios in dinner jackets. Where the toilets flush. Yet even the pampered, as they slip in comfort between the rice fields, must – unless ready to avert their eyes every other minute – retain a recurring image of men pissing against a wall or into an irrigation ditch. Here, among less affluent trekkers, the recurring image differs just a little. Pools of diarrhoea simmering in the heat. I gulp until both lungs are filled with fresh Himalayan air before shutting the door.

My pink and blue bombers are proving effective. All the queasy turmoil in my guts has calmed and these pills would have been cheap at double the price. Throwing my neck back, I stare at (even if I cannot breathe) the polished sapphire sky above this cesspit.

What choice is Daniel making?

I scrunch a handful of orange toilet-paper while wondering if he will keep his underpants on tonight with unParisian prudishness. Are they blue like mine? I study the tan on my calves with pleasure, noting that they are at last as dark as my forearms. My jeans button comfortably. My smugness as I note this seems a harmless vanity. The combination of swimming and walking and Delhi belly has trimmed me so the zip runs up without my breathing in. I kick open the makeshift door and stroll to a boulder where I squat looking towards Zanskar, that hidden kingdom of which Daniel speaks but which I've no time now to discover with – or without – him.

What do I, a fit and suntanned gay now scraping his sandy shoes on middle-age, have to offer Daniel or any other lover? Much – I suppose – what I have always offered. Never having had chorus boy's looks, there have been none to lose. To have invested in honesty in speech and action – or to have aimed to do so (let's hope not only when it suited me) – is at least to have avoided being subject to the law of diminishing returns. To have been lucky with money and position in my late twenties, then watched both snatched from me by the flick of a wheel, has left me with an indifference to both. It is as well I've never craved to be a sugar Daddy. That I seem to this man or that – possibly to Daniel – to embody assurance and understanding continues to astonish me. Is this what Daniel perceives in me and ergo what attracts him? Ian Prote, the mature – if not the old – man of the mountains who'll suggest a safe course along the hazardous path? Just drop your knickers first, please, and pay the randy guru's fee.

Who am I to be certain where any path might lead? At best I can only ever suggest what – in roughly similar circumstances – might untangle a muddle for me. But Daniel . . . what exactly is it that frets this sure-footed young trekker? What prompts him – so assured in public – to snuggle against a comparative stranger in the shadows of a ten-ton truck?

Would you mind, Ian, if I sleep with my head on your shoulder?

That was said. Not supposed. Not recollected with distorting sentiment. Said. A request made in barely accented English fewer than fifteen hours ago. Quite time to find out what decision Daniel has taken.

I wander casually around the perimeter of the outbuildings. At this altitude the lower oxygen content of the air determines it shall be no more than an amble. Sufficient energy to spare, however, for a giggle at myself. There's no further disguising that I'm eager for Daniel's answer. It would be dishonest to pretend that an evening's conversation alone will fulfil me. To concentrate on Bashir's walnut limbs as I drift asleep would be no satisfaction. I'm on the hunt. My quarry's Daniel, naked on that mattress, wanting me.

With charm or luck I shall discover what making love here in the Himalayas demands. Will it be comparable with that frenzied fumbling in a beach hut on the bollock-freezing shores of Loch Lomand with – what *was* his name? No matter. Long ago and not relevant now. Here love will be a slow business. There'll be a light autumnal quality perhaps. A foretaste of old age encapsulated in an hour.

The luggage has been shifted and both bedroom doors are closed. No Daniel. No sherpas. No doubt they're all somewhere on the far side of the restaurant pitching a stores tent or discussing the hiring of local ponies.

I tap the peeling paintwork on the nearer door. Ting opens it. He nods and grins at me and waits. Sherpa number two, whose name sounds like Chin, is behind him unpacking. Sweaters and mess-cans already litter the two single beds. How many times Ting says Hello before I can answer him I really can't swear. I'm singing (though he can't hear me); I'm skating with a proficiency I'll never acquire (though Ting sees me motionless in front of him); I'm diving for the European gay team at the Olympics (even though I have found that the distance between two swimming-boats is a strain).

– Sorry Ting. So sorry . . . Daniel? Has he put our bags next door?

He nods frenziedly. This must be because I've understood the arrangements rather than because he understands the overtones. Or are there gays among the sherpas? Correction: Are there homosexuals who prefer to mitigate the rigours of the sub-zero winters hereabouts with the warmth of friendship? Second correction: Are these sherpas from tribes where bisexuality is an unremarked commonplace? Would Ting perhaps be baffled by even that attempt to classify and define?

Daniel's sleeping bag has been unzipped and thrown across the mattress so that the broad red, white and blue stripes cover our bed like the tricolour of France. For no logical reason I catch myself staring at the window curtain. My grandmother's laughter echoes round me and I hear her saying a blind man could shoot grape-shot through that frayed muslin and not injure the fabric. Tonight I imagine we shall be dazzled by starlight. The stage, as Vince would say, seems very nicely dressed for a romantic little number. Bed in the bush and stars to see, etc, etc. Common sense dictates nevertheless that Daniel might still be motivated by the notion that our two bodies under one cover will generate more heat than two sleeping separately. He must – it has to be conceded – be aware that I am ill equipped for mountain life, having no sleeping bag of my own. None of this remains valid when I notice the tip of a note he's left for me. Both pillows have been plumped together and the half-sheet of paper lies in the cleft between them. Short of yodelling it across the valley, Daniel appears to be doing everything to indicate we should get it together soonest. What then am I to make of his note that tells me he's met an amazingly interesting French girl who is travelling with her lover? How does all this add up? I'm invited to tea for four which he's having served on the verandah outside our window in a few minutes. The man's capacity for reconciling disparate enthusiasms astounds me. I've detected no frightening symptoms of galloping schizophrenia. There's no evidence – as yet – that he intends to join me in the early hours with that omnipurpose knife of his. Stop Press. Grim Report From Himalayas. English tourist pieced together after patient search among Indus tributaries. Monastery spokesperson hints at attempt to deprave novices.

Impossible. Having washed my hands in a tin bowl (does it serve also as a piss pot?) I grimace into the sliver of a mirror that may not have been cleaned since Everest was first scaled. The suntan has obscured a little of that scragginess I've noticed lately at the base of my neck. Let's find out what the amazingly interesting French woman has to say to a mature gay Englishmen.

Our path to the village broadens. Daniel drops back and levels with me as my ankle turns momentarily in a pot-hole. He grips my elbow immediately but I steady myself and beat back an urge to shove him away. A petty resentment. I recognise it as a stupid retaliation. There's no logic in resenting the ease with which Daniel alternates between constructing an intimacy with me and chattering rapidly in French with a freckled teacher from his home city.

– Tell me Ian. Did you also find Hélène attractive?

– Delightful would be my word. I didn't even object to her reminding me just how ignorant I am . . .

– But she didn't say . . .

– I meant implicitly. Buddhism . . . local politics . . . women in India . . . Should have read more so I'd get more out of even this brief glance.

– Maybe you will experience things as profitable for you.

– Sure Danny, We're pretty well down to basics up here. I've started reminding myself that anything's possible.

– Good. Let's hurry. The music's starting again.

In the village square we settle on a dry stone wall to watch some dancing. Daniel assures me this is a genuine harvest celebration. The few tourists who have gathered are welcome to enjoy the rituals, but these are not staged for their benefit and there'll be no soliciting of rupees at regular intervals. He reminds me that Ladakh is a region still untainted by the predatory commercialism of Kashir and Jammu which we've left far behind us.

We wait in the raw heat of the three o'clock sun for another chain dance to begin round the beaten earth of the square. Eight women stand ready. As their graceful progress begins to the accompaniment of drum and clarinet, they move clockwise, each with one (or more) small child clinging to her skirts. Daniel whispers that here polyandry is widespread. Each of the dancers may well have as many as seven husbands. More often than not these are brothers. I question in a coarsely practical way what the Monday to Saturday husbands might devise to amuse themselves when Brother Sunday is enjoying the marriage bed. Daniel shrugs and suggests that most probably they drink.

To me the wearing of any of these costumes that sway gently past would be insufferable in this heat. Our own cotton shirts have been unbuttoned to the waist. The farmers' wives are wearing cassocks of plum or holly-green velvet. Their stovepipe hats are trimmed with purple or turquoise brocade. Each movement of their shoulders accents the melody of the harvest song and sets the rainbow fringes on their shawls fluttering. The dusty little square is transmuted to a kaleidoscope of bright fragments.

We move from the sunlight to the shadow of a small hotel where elderly women are making tea. Their magnificent hats have been extended with great bat wings of astrakhan. In themselves they would be impressive, but then one woman turns and so discloses a tail that falls from the cap on her head to her neck and shoulders. This is weighed down with rough chunks of lapis lazuli. Her neighbour's hat is similar. Daniel probably guesses I'm speculating whether these might be representations of butterflies or dragonflies. He explains that they are flying snakes.

The dance patterns and the melodies so absorb me that I miss Daniel's welcome to a couple who've emerged from the flint and concrete mix of the hotel's façade. More Parisians who'll be perplexed by Daniel's insistence that they must all be very near neighbours?

He turns from some very animated enquiries to rest a hand on my shoulder. These two – a little less attractive than Hélène's lover – are the first of the trekkers. They will have to be walked back to the rest-house so their gear and supplies can be checked. Daniel says he will return for me in half an hour. Without turning I nod. Another dance is starting.

– So sorry, Ian. There was something I wanted to do which took longer than I expected. You were not bored? Excellent. Now we shall go and celebrate for ourselves . . . You must sample some Ladakhi tea.

Whatever delayed Daniel kept him long enough for the sun to have dropped. It catches the snow on the Karocorams now and they sparkle as though garnished with a trillion diamonds. It is possible – but I'll leave Daniel to tell me if he has a mind to – that Hélène and her lover have been persuaded to join the trek to Zanskar rather than continue to Leh. Over tea she and I did agree to pool what guile we have to bribe ourselves onto one of the buses. What's his name? Yves? Yes, Yves . . . seemed acquiescent in his monosyllabic way. If Daniel has charmed them into changing their plans, she'll be livelier company than the two frumpy figures in beige ankle socks who trailed away behind him, past the corner of the village gompa en route for the rest-hut.

As the dancers disperse for tea and the tourists order cokes, Daniel leads me from the square. He asks every child we pass if his or her mother has any Ladakhi tea. The fifth enquiry is successful, and we pick our way carefully behind a small girl through uneven lanes and among half-completed houses that would seem to be constructed of wet fudge. We reach a pine ladder and I follow the little girl up. Fortunately her wicker basket piled with asses' turds has been well cured in the sun. It bobs just above my nose.

We sit with a farmer's wife in her rooftop garden watching the sunset. She is twenty-four. Of her ten children it is number six who guided us here. Number four pours my cup of tea. Daniel feels I should know what I'm about to sip. The brew begins with local tea leaves and boiling water. Not difficult to guess. The regional variation consists in the addition of yak's milk with plenty of sugar and salt. A good dollop of rancid butter with a top-up of finely pounded barley flour and – voilà – we have Ladakhi tea. This is the staple winter diet in these valleys. I smile at our hostess to express what I trust she recognises as pleasure and I take a first mouthful.

There are advantages in an Anglo-Saxon upbringing. Not many perhaps, but we are brainwashed early into supposing the more vile the medicine the more beneficial the effect. I recall this as I attempt to swallow. Only by concentrating on Daniel's chatter about crops and temperatures at this time of year do I prevent myself throwing up.

Daniel informs me I'll be expected to finish five cups. The difficulty is that the second any perceptible gap appears between the rim of the bowl and the greasy warm water it contains, child number four replenishes it. Any one of the old petrol drums from which a few flowers are struggling would be handy. None is within reach. Our hostess – through Daniel – asks how I am enjoying my first taste of tampa. With the equivocation of a diplomat I convey to her that I'm finding it an interesting experience. By tracing with a manic intensity the outline of shadows lengthening along the maize fields below us, I manage to finish a fourth cup. Trying diversionary tactics, I ask for each of the farmers who shares our hostess to be pointed out and named. A vain ploy. Mother is distracted but number four is ready with the metal teapot.

Daniel is well experienced in this ritual. He plunges his hand into the barley flour can and scatters a fistful into the dregs of his tea. Having scoured the inside of his bowl he produces an uncooked dumpling the size of an apricot and flips it into his mouth with the satisfied smile of a connoisseur.

We leave rupees for the children to buy bon-bons. I'd willingly add a couple of the travellers' cheques from my pocket in return for even one of the lemon and lime pastilles I've left in the bedroom. Would it be impolite to ask for a spoonful of the sugar mound on which flies have settled appreciatively?

We clamber in the twilight among stones of a dry valley until – drawing level with the rest-house – we can see kerosene lamps being set on tables in the dining area. In fully fifteen minutes Daniel and I have not exchanged more than half a dozen phrases, yet we are as easy in each other's company as friends who have shared all the years since schooldays. As we approach the verandah I noticed that the wooden benches are already filling with travellers. Individuals and pairs, together with small groups who've arrived too late for the daily buses to and from Leh. Daniel expects that most will have to sleep on the dining-tables. Those like ourselves who have the luxury of a room will not be encouraged to linger over supper. As soon as he has said this, I experience a tug in my stomach muscles that can't be attributed to the cups of tampa washing round. This is the old untameable excitement of the chase. If Daniel can consign his wife and all his fascinating women to the darkness of the ravine for tonight . . . Bashir can dream under the stars a little longer and still find me as affectionate in a different way when we do meet.

Predictably Daniel leads us towards a table which we'll share with Hélène and Yves. As we sit waiting for canned beers, the two frumpy trekkers I saw in the village hesitate for a moment in the shadows by the serving hatch. Daniel calls them over too. They tell us that another couple has shown up and is pitching a tent. He strides away to round them up, leaving me to order for us both.

When I have finished my bowl of coarse vegetable soup, I sit in silence deliberately insulating myself from the rapid Parisian French around me. Why should it be incompatible for me to be thinking of Bashir while preparing to make love with Daniel? His voice breaks through to me. He is asking Hélène if she has never seen him with Charlotte at some local supermarket. In less than an hour the lips that shaped that question will be against my own.

The room is cold. The four stone walls are cold. The beaten earth floor is cold against the soles of my feet, and the door latch – a skein of thin wire which either Daniel or I will bind round a staple – is chilly on the fingers. I listen to him and the sherpas chattering outside the half-closed door while I lie huddled under the sleeping bag. The fingers of my left hand in which I hold a cigarette are close to my face, except for those moments when I must choose between allowing hot ash to fall into my eyes or onto the floor. As the group outside disperses, I squint across at my travelling clock in the corner. Nine o'clock. Daniel has already warned me that we'll need to be up at six.

As he fastens the door, he asks me twice if I've noticed how rapidly the temperature has fallen. The first time I answer with a laugh. My reaction to the cold should be obvious. Having stubbed my cigarette on the base of the candlestick, I have only my nose and forehead protruding from the sleeping bag. It maybe apprehension that prompts his repetition. I reply with a grunt.

It is not Daniel himself that I watch as he begins to undress, but his shadow that is played by our candle across the rough washed wall. Not very tunefully he hums *We Shall Overcome* while I run down a check list of the signals he's been transmitting to me these past thirty hours. The fuzzy circle of his head reappearing when he has pulled off his tartan shirt is that same head I felt snuggling deeper into my shoulder. The warmth of his spikey curls tickling my chest is easily recalled. The jeans from which he hops are those that rubbed against my own kilometre after kilometre.

He breaks the melody in mid phrase to ask if I think we'll be warm enough. What response can there be except that I guess we'll manage?

Rather than glance directly at him to establish whether he is smiling at my assumed complicity, I watch the shadow of his fingers as he folds his jeans. Can he, in say five minutes – ten at most – refute the charge that it was those same fingers that ventured at a snail's gallop along the safety-rail while we swayed at some speed through the valley into Mulbeck?

He balances on one foot to remove his heavy duty socks. His thumb, swollen in shadow to three times its size, gyrated endlessly against my own. He would have difficulty now in convincing me that contact did not also give him pleasure.

Are we now to have a disarming aside that he always sleeps without his undershorts for health reasons? Seemingly not. He turns from me and I abandon his shadow for the substance. He stands on tip-toe in his Boy Blue slip to peer through one of the many slits in the curtaining. His back tapers from well-exercised shoulders to an adolescent's waist. Maybe Daniel is counting on a kick from the slow and teasing removal of that slip.

He turns and it's once again the bulbul smile. With the stylish movement of a jumper he is in the bed and lying close beside me. I wet my forefinger and thumb before snuffing out the candle. Neither of us speaks and I lie on my back beginning to define the dimensions of our room by starlight. The only sound – other than Daniel breathing – is an occasional phrase of Italian or German as couples pass below on their way to the lane of tents pitched round the rest-hut.

When Daniel speaks it is a tiny whisper as though he wishes to offer a secret no one else should share.

– I have enjoyed these days of ours together, Ian. I hope you understand I shall remember them for a long time.

Maybe it is not yet ten past nine but we've only tonight. The hell with ambiguities. My answer must be direct and sup-plemented with some gesture that's not only gentle but firm. Given such a build-up there must be no drifting into uneasy sleep and a rueful swopping of might-have-beens over coffee in the morning. Nor is this game going to be played on Daniel's terms. Well, to be fair, what would appear to be his terms as set out so far. No feigning sleep while indulging in anonymous pleasure. For me that's yesterday or – to be roughly accurate – five thousand yesterdays ago.

Saturday night. Tom chats authoritatively about the athletics championships we've been attending. A good Italian supper and, say, three or four beers. Shoulder to matelike shoulder we share a borrowed bed. Must be past midnight before we lapse to silence. Ten minutes later, Tom – ace of the rugger pack but bloody awful actor – breathes with unnatural regularity. With one long and badly simulated sigh he turns to me so my ready hand is filled with the furred peach of his scrotum. His head is plunged into the oblivion of his pillow.

Tonight Daniel must face his lion's den or rather face me. I've little doubt now that I embody for him something unknown – half welcomed and half feared – that he must meet.

– That's good news . . . I'd agree with you they've been three magic days if we include the picnic and the swimming. Seems logical that we should share our last night.

To counteract any loss of nuance there might be in translation, I thread my left arm under his shoulder. We are now in much the same position as we were hour on bumpy hour in the truck. His head falls once again across my chest as though by reflex. I trust the next few moments won't be transformed to comedy by the hair on my chest tickling his nostrils so that he sneezes.

Time to move on to second base and unmapped territory. My right hand covers his left shoulder and I draw him closer so that I can speak softly only a little distance from his ear.

– This is my way of saying thanks, Danny. I mean for arranging it all so well.

There's no immediate reaction but I do sense his breathing is becoming irregular. Even uncontrolled. He pulls his head back to look at me with our eyes scarcely a handspan apart. His whisper is so small that even the tick of my travelling clock almost obliterates his words.

– Are you homosexual?

He remains exactly where he is lying and waits for me to answer. No wriggling to disentangle himself. No tensing of muscles.

With my index finger I trace his eyebrows and then the

furrows in his forehead.

– Do you often ask questions when you already know the answers?

– But Ian, I did not know. Not until a moment ago when you put both your arms round me . . .

– Listen Danny. Suppose I said that I think you really wanted this to happen . . .

– Wanted this? But why should you say that?

My finger on his lower lip, I itemise examples of the physical affection he has shown since we lumbered out of Srinagar. Although I concede much can be dismissed as unpremeditated, I challenge him to deny stroking my fingers when we were within minutes of Kargil. I hesitate to ask if he's conveniently forgotten the kiss with which I woke him under the first street lights. He could protest it was the jolt of our ten-tonner braking that stirred him.

Having dropped my hand from his lips onto the icy nylon of the sleeping-bag, I wait for Daniel to reply. It is his option now. Either we move apart and sleep or we move closer. Before saying anything, he drops his head again onto my chest. I cannot see his eyes.

– If I tell you I don't remember doing any of these things, I don't think you will believe me . . . Maybe you would understand if I say that my body seems to have been expressing some needs that I have always had, although I myself was quite genuinely asleep . . . or certainly unaware of what my hands were doing . . . does that convince you?

– Mmm . . . not entirely . . .

– Then there is something else – and you must not be angry?

– Try me.

– It is possible that the strong homosexual . . . impulse? Yes . . ?

– Impulse.

– The impulse in you has touched something in me which I have always known existed. It is in everyone, I think.

Heard that before.

– What I can understand, Danny, is that you have been putting out distress signals calling for affection. Holding Ting's hand at the bus station for instance or cuddling up to me in the truck . . .

– But Ting is from a different culture . . .

– Just shut up and let me finish will you? You're putting out these May Day calls because Charlotte and your compulsive need to chat up every woman we've met just aren't enough. For you . . . at the moment. That's no put-down you know. Makes you a bloody sight more human than my dear stepbrother. All he needs is a magnifying mirror.

– Miles. Can I tell you something, Ian, that might make me seem very immoral? I admit that once – earlier this season – I did watch Miles sunbathing. No. I didn't want him but I admitted to myself that some day I would like to experience making love with another man. It would have to be the right man, you understand? And only once so that I would never be worried by homosexuality again. Now what do you think of me?

My yawn is quite shamelessly exaggerated. I'm his man. He's mine and I know he knows it.

– Well . . . good to hear Danny that you're not frantic about proving yourself to be Mister Macho. I can only wish you the best and hope all will go swingingly when you bump into the right guy . . .

He frees himself with the sudden movement of a cat fearing it may be trapped.

– Would you mind if I went for a piss?

– Why should I?

The door remains open. Daniel stands surrounded with stars that shine also on the lepers of Srinagar who dream of a world in which their bodies are wholesome and unblemished. Elsewhere in the darkness teenagers clench their fists against the pain of loneliness and yearn for anyone who will caress and value them as persons. Here on a mountain pass I, Ian Prote, am alone with the archetypal bronzed warrior who has figured in the records of more cultures than our own. As he bounds back across the chilly floor I have one millisecond to consider whether he – the sun god's deputy – will be an exhilarating lover or maybe one who lies inert as all bronze effigies must inevitably do. Having vaulted onto the mattress a second time, he settles my unspoken question by clutching me to him with both arms and with his forehead pressing against my own.

– But I have no need to go one looking for the right man, Ian. But you will have to teach me, for I really do know nothing.

My finger tips define the outline of his shoulders, neck and chest. He grips my biceps tightly as a child does when first experiencing immersion in a swimming pool. His eager breathing is the only evidence of excitement as I explore a path between his pectorals, until I am stroking the hair that fizzes along the waistband of his Boy Blue slip. My lips press softly on his closed eyelids, the colder tip of his nose and finally his lips. I taste the oily sweetness of the salve he smears on them as protection from the mountain winds and sun.

He parts his lips as I kiss him a second time and – at the third contact – both lips and teeth part so that my tongue can begin a private conversation with his own. His belly – responsive to my touch – wriggles so that his slip slides easily away to be lost somewhere below his calves. My fingers forage on progressively around the inner muscles of his thighs.

At last his own hands leave my biceps. They grope to grip my hair, my ears, my neck – anywhere this mountaineer can gain a hold that will allow him to pull my face against his own. The increased urgency with which he rocks our heads from one pillow to the other is the request for which I have been waiting. My fingers close around his genitals and his penis judders to my touch. Its head is broad and curiously smooth. As I fondle the short slenderness of flesh down to its base, I think of the pink lotus of the morning, rising if not from the water – then from the damp, soft weeds of Daniel's pubic hair.

My hand lies angled so that the fingers spread about his balls and my palm folds round his penis. The old charm works. Daniel brings up his knees, and with one kick sends sleeping bag and slip out into the shadows beyond the foot of our bed. He's most certainly no longer a compliant effigy accepting the compliment of love but offering nothing. Imagining perhaps I do not understand his hunger, he grabs my wrist and relocates my hands to offer first his nipples, then his open thighs. Why he should suppose I need encouragement, I've no opportunity to consider. His own mouth is everywhere, consuming me from hairline to ankles with the avity of a beggar let loose on a banquet.

Each of us has some secret cavity. Some particular zone which – discovered by a lover – prompts us to forget all inhibition and abandon ourselves to delight. For some it's ear-lobes. The navel rim for others. In stroking behind Daniel's balls, I have unwittingly found a way of spurring him to ecstasy. When I caress the ribbed seam of darker flesh there, he flails and writhes with such enjoyment that his outstretched fingers tear the ragged window curtain down.

We pause on the very edge of a giggle and Daniel whispers it's as well no one is glancing in. I tell him the stars are getting the best seats, so we might as well give the buggers something to twinkle about. Once he has released the shreds of fabric, he holds me by the neck and draws me to him until I lie across him face to face. He speaks very deliberately so I shall not misunderstand.

– Ian, I want you now much closer to me. I want you to fuck me.

Hasn't the man intimated more than once these past days that he wishes to experience everything? This is no moment to debate the pros and cons. A hero of the Himalayan winters urges me – a passing casual gay – to fuck him. It's to be hoped that Daniel will take this for no more than the consummation of a holiday friendship. I can very well do without being cited in the Paris divorce courts. It must be admitted that I find him . . . compatible? Exciting? Oh the hell with words. I brush my nose against his, Esquimo fashion.

– Will you, Ian?

If this truly is the shapeless monster Daniel has worried about so long – the dark menace in himself with which he's known that he must come to terms – how can I call myself a friend if I refuse to lend a sword for the occasion?

– Pourquoi pas?

Daniel slides from under me. Turning, he humps himself into the air so that I may enter him in the way he's no doubt seen scratched among graffiti in the Paris loos. I hug him. Although I say nothing, he must feel me smiling into his cheek as I depress his shoulders until – relaxed by the gentle massage of my hands, he drops onto the mattress. I only whisper to him that he should turn his face so that it will rest against mine on the pillow.

Too often in a darkened room one lover lies with eyelids scrunched, pretending it is the boy or girl next door who's offering the kisses and not some unsatisfying substitute. Daniel's eyes are on me and I'm glad. No doubt he's known such tenth-rate moments. I'd need more fingers than I now close on his shaking hand to enumerate the times it has occurred to me.

I ride him with affection and delight. Within moments he incites me to plunge deeper and I hold him tighter so that our sweat begins to meld. There is no defining now where Daniel ends and Ian Prote begins. His grip on my forearm loosens and I slide my hand under him to close again on his genitals. My tongue and lips – even the pores on my cheek bones – seem to absorb and re-exude the tang of Daniel's sweat matted in the blond hair at his nape. His kisses on my left wrist turn to bites – half playful and half famished. As I gasp with the increased intensity of the pain, he lifts his face and whispers urgently before thrusting his lips against my mouth.

– Soon Ian . . . Yes, Ian . . . Now.

Conversation has been minimal for some time. Functional would not be quite exact for we shared a quiet laugh. Daniel brought us right down with his observation that only Englishman would have produced a handkerchief just when it was needed. What else has he said? Well he did hiss *shit* when he stood on the stem of his pipe and snapped it while rearranging the sleeping-bag over me. So we share the last cigarette in my pack. From the decisive way in which Daniel stubs it into the candle saucer I suspect he wants to talk before sleeping. Maybe make love again? As he falls back onto the mattress I'm aware he's eased himself a little away from me. He taps my shoulder.

– We should talk now, Ian. But as friends. Of course I still like you very much . . . More than before. Much more. But I'm am certain we shouldn't make love again.

– You are? Worried it might be habit forming?

– I have now experienced love with another man. I am lucky that you are a very gentle person, but we mustn't become a pair like Sally and Jean.

– Danny. Will you just give over and listen? Maybe those two women have a cuddle when one or other of them is really down. Who knows or cares? It's their business. You started pinning roles on them. They sussed it and played the parts you'd cast them in. Finish. They aren't homosexual.

Daniel turns onto his stomach and rests his face on his folded arms. He picked up the impatience in my tone.

– Alright Ian. But you? Have you just being playing a game too because you thought I would enjoy it?

– If you mean have we just made love because I was certain you wanted that, then . . . sure.

– And you still haven't told me if you are really a homosexual.

– Ask me if I'm gay.

– A nicer word?

– Oh . . . more than that. It's late, Danny. Shouldn't we sleep? A little while anyway?

I could certainly sleep. Daniel, still as avid for information as the bulbul is for food, now props himself onto one elbow.

– Soon we must. But tell me, Ian. What is the difference in these two words in English?

– Much the same as the difference in French, I'd guess. Well . . . to put it simply. Homosexuality is a fumble in the dark with someone of the same sex. Even someone without a name . . .

– Not us . . .

– As you say. Not us . . . To be gay is . . . I don't know . . . Yes. To be gay is to walk out in the daylight next morning alongside the person you made love to all night. Well, that's a beginning. The walking together in the morning streets is almost a banner. A badge perhaps that says I have the right to my option too. Oh I'm tired, Danny. Does that make any sense at all to you or am I just cobbling words together?

– I think I follow what you are saying. Isn't it a political act to wear badges and wave a banner?

– What isn't, eh?

– Then tell me, Ian. When you make love do you always play the husband?

– Do I . . ? Your sexual thinking, Daniel, is paleolithic. Alright then. Who made the overtures in the truck, eh? Who chose this bed and not the two singles next door?

– But I told you . . .

– And I'm telling you that I could any moment hug you again and then – without either one of us being able to swear how it happened – you might end up screwing me.

It should be added that each point – as I was making it – was given an extra emphasis. My knuckles jabbed Daniel just below his left nipple. Somewhere around his fourth or fifth rib. No sooner had I finished than he levered himself into a kneeling position to grip me by both shoulders. Deliciously sensual. Chips of ice on my flesh still warm from making love.

– We must never make love again, Ian. You are right. We should sleep now.

– So now who's playing the traditional dominant male, then? Yes. We ought to sleep. I'll agree with you on that. You can tell me a couple of things first just in case we're too busy later. In the morning, I mean.

– What do you want me to tell you?

– One. Will you be telling Charlotte about us?

– But naturally. I have already told you we have no secrets.

– You don't think she might worry that what's happened at

84

last might happen again? Next season? In Paris after you'd had a row?

– You must never feel guilty, Ian. You haven't just converted a married man into a gay revolutionary.

– Guilt doesn't come into it. Married or gay or both isn't second best. Only options. So where's the guilt?

– Question Two?

– Who taught you your climbing and mountaineering?

A haphazard shot may have hit the target. There's no immediate reply from Daniel. He slides back into the bed beside but not against me. I watch him pull up the sleeping bag under his armpits before clasping his hands outside. I suspect I'm about to be offered an edited explanation. Being too sleepy to press for details I am content to listen. Evaluating what Daniel may leave out will pass the time tomorrow in the bus.

– My cousin taught me. I first went with him – that does not mean in any *deuxième* sense – I first travelled with him when I was fourteen. To the Alps.

– And does your cousin come to India too? Like Charlotte?

– Roland was killed near Chamonix during our third winter together.

– That's tragic. I'm sorry. Make this my final question then. What is that dark scar along the side of your left hand?

– That is frostbite. If you can wait until breakfast I will tell you the story. You did say a couple of questions.

– I did, Danny.

He does not object as I pull him so that he lies across me but he does not unclasp his hands. I tug at his left wrist and – when he notices me smiling – he lets me lift it to my face. My lips run tenderly along the edge of his palm. I expect him to turn his head away as I do this, yet – to keep this record fair – I must add that he does not resist when I turn his face towards me and kiss the dimple in his chin.

– Three fine days and an enjoyable night Danny. So far . . .

– I still hope this has not all been a game to you Ian. Sleep well.

– Game? I enjoy games. Just so long as we don't have to win.

Daniel does not snore. Although I was marginally more exhausted in Kargil than I am now I would have been disturbed by snoring. With my eyes closed I begin to concentrate on Bashir's smile. I don't imagine there'll be confusion or pleas of inexperience when we finally get it together in the shady everglades.

Twice as I am losing consciousness I'm startled by Daniel grinding his teeth as he sleeps. Well, there's no perfection outside a gallery of classical sculpture . . . If there is, I've long since lost the urge to chase it.

THE GARDEN is bright and tranquil. Zinnias bloom knee-high around me and dahlias broad as dinner plates stir in an occasional breeze above my head. I read here in the shadow of a guest house wall before the heat becomes too aggressive. Between noon and three in the afternoon I eat a samosa and stare south-west towards the Karocorams. From time to time I lick my fingers before scribbling another postcard. There are hazards in sending cards. Unscrupulous managements – though I think not here – do tend to accept them, then pocket the stamp money before trashing the cards. It would be difficult to check this snippet of tourist mythology for there can be few who regularly return to Leh.

The card uppermost on my lap is not of Ledakh. Like so many of those I have snatched up while commuting between the bank and the bus station it is of a landscape somewhere to the south. Most certainly this under-exposed view of a rickety bridge is no reproduction of that which I crossed two days ago in a B-class bus. There's no placidity about the turgid Indus and none of those lush colours in the bleak terrain we traversed.

The card I have just addressed, however, has on the obverse a Ladakhi farmer grinning from beneath a festive hat garnished with an extravagance of wild flowers. By Ascot standards it would be garish. Worn on a gay pride march in London or Sydney it might do something to counteract charges that such events seem set on expiring in respectability. There are hats such as this sold along the broad main street of Leh for around three English pounds.

Having considered lumbering myself with half a dozen hats as presents for friends, I dismiss the notion in favour of apricot sponges. This may appear a bizarre alternative unless it is understood that the guest house in which I'm staying would seem also to serve as the town's bakehouse for apricot sponges.

As I wonder how well sponges might travel, a motherly figure – plump and with strands of coppery hair – scuttles up the path towards me from the stream. She is exactly on cue. Before she levels with me, I realise her hair appropriately enough is not coppery at all. To be precise it is more overstewed apricot. She pauses – somewhat breathless – and extends her arms in a lavish operatic gesture.

– The Queen requires one of my sponges for tomorrow afternoon. What is to be done? You must know – *I* know – everybody knows the electricity can fail here at any moment this evening. In every restaurant they will tell you my sponges are the most delicate concoction. What must I do? Should I decline do you think?

There's no manic glitter in her glance as she waits for advice. Merely anguish. Despite my tendency to doze in the early afternoon heat, I am very surely awake and the flapping figure in front of me is not something that has eluded the margins of Alice in Wonderland and waddled into my daydream. I try soothing her into coherence.

– One should decline a royal invitation only for the very soundest of reasons. I haven't read a paper for weeks you know . . . Tell me – has the Queen of England arrived early for this Commonwealth Conference that's being planned?

Once again I rediscover the disadvantages of not having spent rainy evenings back in London poring over guide books. It has to be explained to me that Leh still has a royal family and that the present Queen sits in the Delhi parliament. She lives in an unpretentious little place just along the valley (more dramatic gestures indicate the site) with her daughters. One of the Princesses does some nursery teaching and potty-training in the same voluntary school as that in which the sponge-baker works each morning.

– So how am I to bake something fit for royalty in these conditions?

The only constructive suggestion I can offer is that she starts three sponges at half-hour intervals when the generators come on at sundown. The whole process – I improvise – should be considered as a cross between a relay and a handicap race. The best top and the best base can then be sealed with the inevitable apricot jam and forwarded to the palace. She claps her hands and scuds away as one inspired towards the kitchen, pausing only at the corner of the wall to promise me a huge helping of the runner-up either for supper or to take with me on the bus tomorrow – if I ever get away.

She is an astounding woman. This morning I learned (but not from her) that she was hounded from Germany as a child with her Jewish mother. Each summer she comes here to Leh and works for six weeks. In a few days she, too, will be returning to England where she cooks in the kitchens of a residential school for handicapped teenagers. She speaks English with a Scandinavian accent and her German too leads people to think she's a holidaymaker when she returns each Christmas to Köln. There is no bitterness in her for the young in what was once her native city. Only for some of the elderly, who she insists would vote again as they once voted half a century ago.

As I pick up my postcard of the river bridge once more and jot the date, she reappears. There's a further dilemma. Would it be presumptuous to outline a crown in the centre of the sponge? I imagine the Queen – and I say this – would be delighted, but I do add a caution that it might be prudent to surmount it with a star rather than a cross. The cook relaxes and I rather hope she'll leave me to scribble my cards. She doesn't move so I try to change the conversation to a less immediate topic.

– Aren't the flowers here magnificent? Not just the garden but along the road sides and right across there along the slopes . . .

She nods forcefully but when she speaks anguish returns to her voice. Wretched European exporters – or so she tells me – are now dumping on Third World farmers all those pesticide sprays which they are forbidden to market at home. Her arms flamboyantly sweep the valley and the gompas glinting on the hillsides.

– Tell me then . . . can you see one cornflower? Even one? They are the first victims, you know . . .

I can see two. They are no smaller and no larger than Daniel's eyes.

Does it have to be here on the tarmac of the road we have been sharing these past days? So be it then. We stand surrounded by a chorus of tourists waiting as I do for the bus. There are military walk-ons too, who smoke and joke and piss while waiting for the green flag that will signal their morning convoy on its way. It isn't difficult to perceive that Daniel wishes me to initiate a goodbye hug. How will he equate that public statement with his flirting and chattering with Hélène? That's his business. It's certainly none of mine whether they have or haven't swopped addresses. She sits on my baggage stacked beside their own and smiles at both of us. Does she know we shared more than a double bed? There's only one certainty at this moment. For Daniel and I to split with a handshake would be ludicrous.

He whispers. His voice is so small that I have to listen intently or lose what he is saying in the revving of a distant army truck.

– I wish Ian . . . I really wish I could give you the affection you need. With the beginning of a laugh that I trust will not bruise his sincerity, I ease Daniel back to arm's length.

– Come on now. There's more kindness than logic in that. How sure are you, Mr Bulbul, it isn't yourself you're talking about again?

This is no time to begin a discourse on what I've said. I shall not be writing to him and though he could check my London address in the houseboat register when he returns from Zanskar, I've no expectation that my name will be added to his New Year's card list.

– But surely, Ian, everybody needs the very special affection of one other person?

– There's a cue for a song if I ever heard one, Danny. Now listen. It was fine and good making love. Right? If you look over your shoulder, though, you'll see the door's open and the floor's been swept in what was, but isn't now, our room . . .

– You could change your mind. Again. You could come with us. I wouldn't care what the other trekkers . . .

– But the season would still end in a couple of months. The passes will snow up. We'd still have to take our different routes to Europe . . .

Two fingers of my right hand tap the tanned and hairless sternum above his open shirt. Can I convey to him in ten seconds what I want him to understand?

. . . You contradict yourself more than I do, Daniel. Who said after we'd made love – the first time I mean – that we must revert to being friends? Here we are a few hours on and you're offering a holiday affair. Where would that get us? . . . Passionate reunions at Calais . . . regular monthly bookings in a chilly Dover Hotel?

– And that would not be sufficient for you, Ian? You prefer to forget me when you return to London, eh? Finally people are not as important in your life as your marches and your posters against bombs and fascism and all those other fine causes you have referred to?

– Now, now. No more important . . . and no less. Remember when you tore down that rag of a curtain last night? If we'd been less absorbed in each other's pleasure we could have stood at that bare window and stared and stared . . . Know what we just might have been able to make out? The very same pretty starlight that seemed to have switched itself

*on especially for us would also have shown us warheads still being
manufactured . . . cripples still begging. I just don't see how we can
switch off any more than those stars . . .*

*We hug and both know that it is for the last time. Daniel's head
against my own is nearer the road. I hear army corporals clambering to
their driving seats and can guess the three daily buses bound for Leh are
nosing among the rocks ten kilometres down the road.*

*– Ian . . . Ian . . . I could not have imagined until a few days ago
that such a friendship was possible between two men . . . It is an
experience I do not wish to share with anyone else . . .*

*– Cut the sentiment Danny or you'll blur my view. Travel safe
through the passes . . .*

My view across the valley in which Leh rests is not blurred. I
realise suddenly that the motherly cook – having found me
uncommunicative – has slipped away to her sponge mixture
once more.

I scan the rooftops of this green oasis huddled in the
Himalayas. If one forgets the airport – not difficult with one
flight a day and sometimes not that – and if one ignores an
occasional army patrol through the main street, Leh cannot have
changed much for centuries.

At breakfast the woman opposite me asked if I didn't agree
that the views are breathtaking. The description is doubly
accurate. At ten thousand English feet no one romps through the
brief dusk to the Tourist Reception Centre. Alone or in
straggling pairs and trios newcomers trudge from the setting-
down point by what's probably the only traffic circle in Ladakh,
to a badly signposted hut. On arrival Hélène, Yves and I
dropped our baggage in the doorway and joined others seeking
accommodation. Very different from Kargil, where bus passengers are solicited with cards and invitations through the open
windows before the engine has been switched off. In Leh it's
agreed by tourists at the bank or over supper tables that group
travellers fare better than individuals since they've invariably
been prebooked. Low or even zero rating for the Tourist Centre
is also the consensus.

Surprise! Surprise! The assistants – guessing full well that
every traveller's priorities must be a wash, a meal and a bed –
were just out of free maps and brochures. For the equivalent of
an English pound, the one remaining brochure that happened to
be under the counter could be provided. I, among many who

refused to buy without a receipt, pushed through to consult a wall map. Having scribbled the names of three guest houses, I asked how far these were. The mute response was a shrug and an imprecise wave out into the lane, which was lit by oil lamps on the market stalls and in the windows of a couple of curio shops.

My efforts to pronounce the name of the guest house at the top of my list weren't very productive. Shrugged shoulders. But at least there were smiles again. I needed a bath and I needed a meal. Hélène and Yves decided to try for a cheap pad back towards the bus station, but I was tired.

As I was about to question a fourth stallholder, I heard distinctly occidental singing drift from the direction of a stream dribbling across the road at the lower end of the market. Greg and Vince. Had to be. Loaded as I was with bags, they still compelled my attention. Whatever it was they were parodying now, it would be a stark contrast to the mountain jerseys, candies, bright strings of beads and folksy hats piled on the stalls. A desire to plod on and listen overcame my wish to linger by a snake-charmer.

By the stream a cosmopolitan crowd was clapping to the rhythm these itinerant actors were imposing. Their early evening aperitif – as I supposed it to be – ran (more or less):

> Now I am a gompa gawper
> From Nashville Tennassee
> I've some tourist trash
> And a pocket of hash
> And three Leicas on my knee

Fortunately – to be selfish about it – this turned out to be the final encore of their sunset cabaret. The crowd began to drift and I was able to ask whether they knew where the guest house – that is *this* guest house – might be.

As they recognised me, I was welcomed with a potted *commedia dell'arte* mime. Tears were simulated with onions borrowed from a vegetable stall as props. They apologised that their own hotel was full but Vince persuaded a twelve-year-old to guide me here. There were more apologies that they were both committed to supper with a woman who teaches in a school in East London. Their warning that I would fritter half my time in Leh trying to change money or trying to get out has proved irritatingly accurate. Three hours at the bank is average and regular visits for anything up to three days at the bus station not unusual.

Sure of a small guide who'd not leave me until I found a room I rallied and shared cigarettes with Greg and Vince. When I reminded them that an hour back the bus did pass a turning to the airport, they giggled. Greg told me the lounge there bulges perpetually with those who cannot contemplate the hazards of the road a second time. Other than for leisured travellers, it might as well not exist. Twice or even three times a week weather conditions preclude take off. One might have paid for a flight – even confirmed it – but if the plane doesn't fly then it's down to the tail of the standby list. This morning at the bank I heard there are one hundred and fifty-seven people waiting on standby.

Greg seemed to be overstating the dangers of the journey. He could only be basing what he said on hearsay and I told him so. Vince commented – flicking the butt of his cigarette archly – that maybe I didn't spend much time looking out of the truck. This instantly developed to an interchange of astounded eyebrows and tongues rotating in cheeks between the two of them. Vince asserted he knew all the time that Daniel had a sponginess under his crunchy macho coating. I expected a pay-off from Greg and was not disappointed. In his experience – he suggested playfully – men with pointed faun ears like Daniel have the hots for anything that's walking. He was sure Danny was *e'en now* shagging a yak. Although I laughed at this, I found I'd placed a hand on the twelve-year-old's shoulder and felt the need to be alone for a while. There's no doubt Greg registered all this, for he comforted the boy with a stage whisper that the English gentleman wouldn't have a funny turn and want to play naughty games, because he was too tired for anything other than the recollection of his bare night on a mountain.

I have not met either of them since my first evening here. They've not been at the bus station to which I've trudged three times so far. Nor in the gompa, where I listened to monks chanting prayers for those about to climb through the foothills towards Tibet and China. Perhaps they did slip their shoes off and sit cross-legged among other tourists, long after I'd excused myself with smiles in the direction of the novice who was about to start refilling our bowls with Ladakhi tea.

Here in the tranquillity of a summer garden I am ready to concede that the journey has done something to change me. I am glad it was undertaken, though I'll not go along with those who speak of it as an experience akin to mystical. For me indisputably the road by which I return will not be the road I travelled from Srinagar to Leh. Should this updating of the old Greek quote lead to some philosophic stock-taking? Maybe. To me, this idle thought in a Himalayan context suggests instead a solution to the problem of presents for friends. Winter gloves. Half a dozen pairs from a market stall.

Each time I have passed them on my way to the main street I've noted something familiar. The old Greek Key pattern is knitted in a band across the yak's wool palm. A cream motif on a chocolate ground. This might well be a confirmation of that argument among anthropologists which suggests the confluence point of European and Asian cultures is right here in Northern India.

Time to post my cards, buy the gloves and make for the bus station. Again. My lazier self mocks that it might have been better to have stumbled along with Daniel into Zanskar. All the tiresome details of haggling for bus and hostel places could have been unloaded on his willing shoulders. Even the most inhospitable rock ledge would have been transmuted to a Hilton each night under his sleeping bag.

As I fasten the garden gate behind me and pick my way across boulders alongside the stream, I confront a naked shepherd boy washing his hair. When he notices me he smiles, not at all coyly. His eyes are not as inviting as Bashir's.

ONE *Super De Luxe Air-Conditioned Tourist Class* bus speeds across the flat wide valley leading from Leh. In the ochrous light of early morning I yawn and offer a silent cheer for passenger power. Without it (or more particularly without the cool determination of a school teacher from East London) I – plus the dozen others now dozing behind me – would very likely be converging yet again on the bus station arguing rather unequally with Mr Bakshish for a place on any kind of four-wheeled vehicle that might be leaving for the south.

Does he guess his photograph will never appear in the travel columns of dailies from Oslo to Darwin, whatever the Aussie freelance threatened last night? No doubt he measured us by his own yardstick and calculated that we, once quit Leh, would leave later tourists either to play the system or do as we have done – combine and overcome it. The corrupt wretch was happy to pose by a Dutch political correspondent despite her warning that she undertook to make him a byword for infamy and double-dealing.

Mr Bakshish can't – or so I suppose – have faced many groups who've produced a list of those waiting for bus places in order of arrival. And kept a copy. This seemed the most practical course for an encounter with a man who – having opened the ticket kiosk for twenty minutes last night – sold two token tickets to the waiting crowd and then swore all places were taken for today. We've Ellen to thank that we're here – a polyglot assortment of Australians, French, Italians and at least one German – making for Kargil. She insisted we stopped offering individual protests and listed us with our arrival times.

Have there been tourists earlier this season or last who've set sentries throughout the night to watch for buses arriving? I doubt it, and I'd be more sceptical if told it was quite usual for angry visitors to despatch a mini-delegation in search of the

Chief of Police and the Tourist Board Manager. I'd certainly be astounded if Mr Bakshish at this very moment is gnawing his nails at the thought of twenty-five letters of protest about him arriving in New Delhi. The scathing articles for local papers will never develop from a few jottings on the backs of our maps and guide books . . .

The driver nudges me and explains we are now passing under the Nimmu Gate. We pass through this huge boulder on a narrow track hacked in the rock itself. A sign hammered onto the rock face isn't without humour. *Go Gently Round My Curves.* It's to be hoped our driver will continue to follow that injunction as we head for the Indus escarpment.

We went more than abrasively round the curves of Mr Bakshish. He's probably more puzzled than abashed that the perks he's come to expect as part of his job haven't – for once – been forthcoming. This was the explanation offered me last night by the guest house owner when I told him of our difficulties at the bus station. We have in innocence ignored the conventions. When in trouble in Kashmir – and need it be added Bakshish is a Kashmiri – show the brown flag, i.e. offer ten rupees. If in dire trouble try the red flag. Fifty rupees. Had any one of us known this, there's small doubt we'd have been on one of yesterday's buses or even the day before that. By playing this convention the locals have been avoiding six-hour queues since the Kashmir and Jammu Transport Company's vehicles first nosed over the passes into Leh eight years ago.

And before that? How could one doubt there was a perennial scarcity of mules until sufficient rupees had changed hands to have bought the poor beasts twice over? Once back south of the Koji-la it would probably have been quicker and more economical to have eaten the brutes than have tried to sell them.

All but two of my fellow passengers have now slumped down in their seats and are sleeping. We were called in our hotels and guest houses and rest-huts at five this morning. By the stream where Greg and Vince entertained a crowd and where yesterday a shepherd boy bathed in the sunlight, about a dozen sheep were grazing on lush grass in the first light. I heard a boy's voice calling goodbye. The same young shepherd – clothed this time – was sharpening a butcher's knife on a flat stone.

Legally I shouldn't be on this bus. Having paused to buy tiny mountain apples from a Ladakhi farmer in the shadow of a gompa, I arrived almost last at the bus station. We'd agreed on six as a rendezvous, yet others were obviously even more sceptical of Mr Bakshish's offer than I.

All the passenger seats were already occupied and I am perched – quite against all regulations – on the Bus Inspector's seat in the driving cabin.

– But you'll love sitting there. Greg and I are quite convinced you're not really musical at all . . .

The actors are with us. The only two who are not sleeping. Just how they secured the two front seats without being involved in our passenger power movement I intend to find out whenever we stop. Maybe they paid a backhander at their hotel and Bakshish collected his split on it. How much of this country runs on palm grease? If the ferret-like Bakshish counts on ten rupees per passenger, that's four hundred per bus. Three buses a day equals twelve hundred. And seven working days a week. Eight thousand four hundred? Eight hundred English pounds or more a week? Can't be. Unless he has every official in the city of Leh soothed into acquiescence and complicity . . .

Suppose I can make Bashir understand this when we meet. Suppose, that is, my mime is adequate and that he does understand – not just nod enthusiastically to be pleasant and friendly. Will he shrug? Would it be sentimentality on my part to imbue him with qualities of integrity he may not have? Why, oh why, Ian Prote, is there any need tomorrow – no – the day after tomorrow – to mention the matter at all, when all Bashir wants and all you should want is an unruffled afternoon in the everglades where affection can be celebrated as both intend?

WE HAVE a thirty-minute break at Khalsi. Our vegetable omelets were ordered fifteen minutes ago and Greg promises he'll go and cook them himself if they've not appeared by the time Vince has returned to our table under the apricot trees. Greg asks if I'm silent because I'm thinking about Daniel. I correct him.

– Now I wouldn't want to pry . . .

– Of course not, Greg . . .

– You did say though that you'd helped Daniel to sort out a deep-seated fear, or as you put it picturesquely – you helped him face his monster. Yes?

– Roughly.

– So what's yours?

– My monster? Oh, maybe conquering a fascination I've had with sunny action men like Daniel . . .

– Balls and you know it. Sex is no problem for you. We've watched you – Vince and I – you don't eye each passing crotch in a famished way. Either you're hiding your monster in the mountains from yourself or you've not had the encounter yet. But Ian baby, whatever it may be . . . sex it ain't. Here's Vince, bopping along, dripping typhoid from every toe-nail. Bathing in that sewer of a stream. Too much. I'm going to collect our food. Think about monsters and tell me later.

But I don't. The view along this little street lined with quick lunch cafes leads on up the Indus escarpment. There are pinpoints of light like minute explosions, as the midday sun catches metalwork on vehicles crawling towards that sweep of the pass where I left Daniel.

– *So you're both near neighbours of Danny in Paris?*

Hélène and Yves stare first at me and then at each other. They appear puzzled. We have found three adjacent seats on the B-class bus and have relaxed, knowing we shall make Leh by sunset. We are exchanging boiled sweets and easy chat. Hélène leans towards me across the aisle.

– I find all this very strange. We were saying – Yves was saying to me – that you Ian and Daniel must be very close friends. He was so anxious to leave us all last night and share the last few hours with you.

Yves watches me with more of an answer than a question in his eyes. He knows Daniel and I slept together. This could explain why he didn't bristle with macho hostility during supper as Daniel endlessly monopolised Hélène. Did he – noting no doubt the casual intimacy that had developed between Daniel and me – presume further that we might be habitual lovers? I smile slightly at him in confirmation of whatever fiction he might be constructing.

– We got well. Leave it at that. But Hélène, you still haven't told me how well you know him . . .

– Neither of us has ever met him before. Naturally I know the quarter where he says he lives. We often use the supermarket he mentioned but I have never seen him and we didn't recognise the photograph of . . . Charlotte? Yes, Charlotte – his wife . . .

If Hélène has begun to question what Daniel purports to be, she may doubt the jaunty heterosexuality he projects. Yves certainly does. His question confirms it.

– Did he also show you this photograph of his wife?

– Oh we talked about her. I didn't see any photograph. I accepted his word because he seemed – well . . . honest . . . kind. Generous too. D'you know, he insisted that I pay only fifty rupees towards two days travel with accommodation and food thrown in.

Yves lights a cigarette but doesn't offer the pack. He exhales and while following the smoke as it ascends, jabs a comment at me.

– Well that was kind, of course. He was perhaps being generous because he was concealing something . . .

– I didn't see it that way possibly because I wasn't doing a character assessment. Just sharing some time with a friend. Anyway, don't most of us conceal private things about ourselves from people we've only just met?

Yves doesn't comment immediately. We have all settled back against the hot leather hoping a breeze might slip in from the windows. The air here is sweet, not – as in Delhi – thick on the tongue and with the stench of over-baked towels in a municipal bath house. He murmurs something in Hélène's ear that causes her to grin and nudge his ribs with her elbow.

– Sometimes in the night, Ian, we all have an urge to share our private terrors with a human being we can trust to be discreet, eh?

He knows. For whatever purpose, he has been assessing Daniel.

As Vince sits down opposite me he throws three small plastic bags of fresh apricots on the wooden table.

– Got them half the price along the road. They rip us off something rotten at these places . . .

– You can say that? After all your cracks about exploitative tourists?

– Look around you, honey. If you were tramping through farmyard shit you wouldn't flaunt a little Savile Row number would you? This is an easy valley, take it from me. Like all farmers they keep their best drag and trinkets in the old cedar wood chest. I come from farming country. Take it from me and don't misplace your sympathy. What – Greg, dear heart – are those?

– Omelets for all. A little sad but no doubt nourishing . . .

They are. We clean the plates, then go inside to pay and to collect bottles of iced fruit drinks for the bus. As we wait in its shade for the driver to return, Greg asks me once more about my monster.

– Still thinking about it but I'll let you know tonight in Kargil. In a way I can't easily explain, you two might be . . . maybe not leading me to it but . . . how can I put it? Clearing the ground for my combat with it? That'll do for me, though it might amaze you.

– Another satisfied customer, Vince?

– Could be, Greg. At least we've jogged him out of smug complacency. What do you do for bread, Ian?

– I'm an overpaid clerk who's offered modest comfort and pleasure in return for not asking too many awkward questions. And you what do you both do? You don't seem to hand round the begging bowl after each finale.

– Oh, but we do in the posh joints. Where they can pay conscience money we take it. Our wants are simple.

– Too right, Vince. Bugger the protestant work ethic. Observe any Moroccan market lad for a few days. That'll cure you. Sufficient unto the day is the grafting thereon. Enough for bed, a meal, a smoke and an extra performance if you want new shoes . . .

– You should try it, Ian.

– Maybe I should. Where are you from?

– Does it matter? Nobody asked me which maternity block

I'd prefer. What's all the nationalism bit, anyway? Everybody's seen where that leads to. Talking of which, Ian . . . you were getting a slap down as we got out here from old Herr Kraut, weren't you?

The driver has slipped into the bus behind us and the horn is blaring, so I can only yell that I'll tell them both in Kargil.

The Australian photographer continues with his close shots of children still plying small bags of apricots. Another tourist bus has drawn up in front of our own. Our driver continues to thump his horn but the bus is only half full. Ellen, standing behind me in the door-frame to the driving cabin, surprises me. She shouts into my ear asking why I'm laughing. I explain that despite years dedicated to rejecting control by imposed stimuli I might as well be one of her more compliant pupils. One blast of the driver's horn and I've settled in my seat for the afternoon. She too nods, then jerks her head back slightly to ask if I've discovered how Greg and Vince managed to slip onto the bus without any of the hassles the rest of us have experienced. I tell her that it really matters less each hour but I promise to ask them at supper.

The bus has pulled out and is moving along the street before the stout German business man heaves himself up in a shower of sand through the open door. It is my intention to slide down as far as I'm able and sleep for an hour. Through the side window I watch the afternoon traffic preceding us up the Indus escarpment. Each vehicle spaces itself at a safe distance behind its predecessor. I trace the progress of a truck painted with green and white stripes. It disappears round a curve to the left and after a minute or so re-emerges a little higher on the mountain side and begins to edge to the right. The immensity of the scarp dwarfs us all to detailed models in a toy shop wonderland.

Mr Bakshish cavorts in front of me. If I creep to the back of the bus station office, to catch him selling tickets to his friends while refusing one to me, he is in the doorway grinning. When I try to fox him by idling along the side wall, then suddenly vaulting onto the ledge of a side window, he hisses in my face that there are no buses and will be none for weeks. I wait until all other tourists have wandered despondently away. I must leave Leh. Bashir is waiting and all fellow-feeling for others who are stranded becomes unimportant. I hide in the shadow of a tea stall until the forecourt is deserted. Bakshish is sniggering in the door-frame. He is about to close up for the night. When the aperture between frame and door is no wider than my head, I charge. The impact on my shoulder is as though the door has been made of reinforced steel. I grab his neck and demand he finds me a bus. He seems terrified and produces one no larger than a child's toy. Before I can ask if he thinks me a fool, he raises it and cracks it down on my skull. It is not his laughter that wakes me.

The hysteria is not my own. One of me fellow passengers is screaming. Others are shouting. Not fully conscious, I find I'm dabbing my scalp very cautiously. The skin has not been broken by the force with which I've been flung against the body-work of the bus. No toy bus in a dream, but our bus. I glance through the window to my left and feel I shall vomit. Instead I slide very slowly to my right until sitting almost on our driver's lap. I do this without explanation and without daring to breathe. Any sudden redistribution of our total weight, I'm convinced, will topple us over whatever minimal verge there may be between our wheels and the chasm which drops to the Indus, gurgling hundreds of metres below us.

A supply truck overloaded with fruit and vegetables has finally broken down. I watched it grinding along in front of us before I dozed off. Three men are now placidly squatting on the road under its tailboard while examining the rear off-wheel. One is so close to our bonnet that I can count the folds in his scarlet turban. He appears unperturbed that – to avoid flattening him – we have braked so violently as to have stopped within millimetres of extinction. Our driver seems quite unshaken. He shouts over his shoulder above the hubbub that we should all get out and stand in the shadow of a quarried alcove by the rear of the vehicle. The passenger door opens behind me. I swallow and nerve myself to glance round, knowing that all I shall see is a rectangle of sapphire blue air.

How the others clamber out I neither know nor care. Vince and Greg wait until last and I beckon them. My throat is dry and my tongue feels burnt and swollen as though I had chain-smoked a pack of twenty cheap cigarettes. My hands twitter like pampas grass in a gale. I explain to them I cannot move along whatever edge exists without their assistance. No threats, no promises, not the entreaties of ten dozen Bashirs could make me look into that chasm.

Greg goes first. He assures me cheerfully there's more than a whole pace between the chassis of the bus and the broken stone verge. Vince grips my wrists as I step down back first onto shale. I begin to shuffle sideways alongside the vehicle, reading each badly painted letter on the bodywork. As I start to spell out Jammu and Kashmir, I find I'm breathing more naturally. The rear cannot be too far. As I begin to congratulate myself that my heart is resettling somewhere nearer my fifth rib than my gullet, Vince observes there's plenty of room for a stroll if one happens to be an ant. I find myself screaming at him.

– Shut fucking up, will you? Who asked you intrude on my sodding holiday anyway?

Perhaps they realise I'm close to fainting. Half conscious and – let's admit it – half hysterical, I'm carried the remaining distance and lowered against one of the rocks littering the alcove.

The Australian photographer is forcing his brandy flask against my teeth with the repeated assurance that I'll not vomit if I can swallow just one mouthful. I do so and begin to take in the scene. The German – whose business may or may not be geology – is yelling abuse at our driver. Ellen pummels her fists against the man because he is insisting that the wheel be handed over to someone who knows the blind bends along the escarpment. Greg is simulating an attack of the vapours, thus giving Vince the chance to waft a fan of peacock feathers (ten rupees Delhi, twenty rupees Srinagar, but five rupees in Leh market) under the twitching bulb of his nose. Immediately Greg becomes aware of Ellen's exasperation with the German he yells that maybe Mein Herr would care to take over, since he's claimed expertise in most of the topics they've been chatting about in the bus. In so far as I can interest myself in anything other than my own gibbering terror, I have to concede Greg has a point. I had intended to tell him at supper of the put-down I was given as we arrived in Khalsi. All I'd offered was a casual pleasantry that we appeared to be passing among rocks rich in copper seams. If green surface stains in Zambia indicate the presence of copper, then why not in North India? I was informed that I knew nothing of geology. The German's face then was merely stiff with arrogance. It is now white with fury. Is it possible that such anger may be his personal mask that conceals fright?

– C'mon, will yer?

The Australian thrusts his flask at me a second time and I swallow not one, but three gulps before he can remove it. I grab him by both forearms. Rubbing my unshaven chin on one, I promise I will buy him doubles all evening in Kargil if we do manage to find a backstreet bar that keeps brandy under the counter. He raises his eyebrows.

– Sure you don't mean *if* we make it?

– When. Keep saying when . . .

I neither know nor care how convinced the photographer is by my hysterical insistance that we shall reach Kargil safely. What are my words but the verbal equivalent of our German fellow traveller's stiff features? Each hides his fear differently but it is a similar fear.

Although I strive to rest calmly, trying to concentrate only on the rawness of the brandy against my lips, our near catastrophe has reduced me to doubting far more than the likelihood of reaching Kargil. I do not have the kind of courage that can contemplate how near I have been to nothing more than a pathetic mound of mud and guts in the chasm. Instead – for no reason I can attribute to common sense, far less logic – I lie on the shale pondering the motives and the authenticity of those who've shown me nothing but kindness.

The two actors for instance. Greg first. Is that his name? What does this man with a face as white and greasy as grandma's suet pudding want of me? What are those two brown raisin eyes of his searching for, here in the Himalayas? And his wizened companion who calls himself Vince – what's his racket? By any yardstick it's kindness to describe his features as gargogular. His acting has the competence of fringe theatre, so – what's his game? Heroin? Cocaine?

Even as I note my need to find out more of heavy drugs, Daniel's face swims before me bringing fresh misgivings. Indeed, I did share a night with everyone's embodiment of the guy next door. No more than a pleasant holiday encounter in an unusual context. Or so I thought until a young Parisian couple started a minor earth tremor with their doubts about his background. Their questions – shaped like eyebrows raised in disbelief – appeared to imply they suspected his name might not be Daniel at all. Is he perhaps also an actor – more polished than the other two? Not even French?

That he is – or so he let me suppose – an excellent mountaineer is not the point. Is it feasible that Daniel uses trekking as a cover to revisit this region where India, Pakistan and Afganistan . . . even China . . . meet? Where better than the ancient trade routes for swopping not silks and spices, but the spicier morsels of military intelligence? Or industrial intelligence, which seems as valuable as any other. Is it ludicrous to wonder whether Daniel – or whatever his given name may be – is a Russian? Until recently of course it would be. Yet wasn't there a television documentary that outlined the training course for the KGB's Quiet Ones? Young Russians learning to pass as gay.

. – I am your new instructor fresh from a fact finding emission in the West. As of this instant I have to tell you that all wrist-flapping and signet rings and lilac cravats are out. Finish. This morning, comrades, we begin to practice cloning by numbers so that you can penetrate – my little joke, niet? – any of these degenerate clubs. Watch out for the one they have dared to call The Tchaikovsky. Now . . . are you ready? One: Smooth the moustache. Two: Grip your tartan shirts. Grip not strip, Dmitri . . . I mean Daniel. Grip it.

Has Daniel even gone to Zanskar? E'en now he could be in one of those army trucks which have no doubt reached the top of the escarpment while my own attention on happenings here in our alcove has weakened.

Still disturbed by doubts – however fanciful – I force myself to listen to the Italian student who has been asking the driver when we can expect to move.

– We are to rest here. For about fifteen minutes. The driver has told me that when the three men have finished changing their . . .

Ellen helps his vocabulary.

. . . exactly. Thank you. When they have changed their wheel they will help us to push our own bus back onto the road. We shall then continue to Kargil.

An American woman, whose travelling companion is nearer forty than twenty, puts up her parasol before protesting that the men in our group should not sit back and wait for the locals to do the heavy work for us. The said travelling companion – too rounded and succulent for my taste – puts her down with a phrase about sexism. He is unnecessarily terse so maybe like me he's still scared shitless. The German mutters that having paid for luxury travel he'll not sweat like a pig behind a bus for anyone. Will I? If I'm allowed to shove from the near side and so be guaranteed something substantial between me and oblivion, then surely I will.

Without one consultative glance – or so it seems to me – Greg and Vince leave the boulder on which they've been perching and move towards the unoccupied centre of the alcove. We are about to be involved in another of their performances which may or may not be improvised:

Well, well, well. Time to get acquainted, fellow travellers. This is my bosom pal Rosie Sherbert and I'm Pineapple Rita . . .

Or Reet, as she's happy to be called by any stray democrats who might have infiltrated the nicer type of touring group. Not as fussy as yer used to be, are yer duck?

Ellen is already laughing. She is in her late thirties and must recognise, even in this opening banter, a combination of the unsophisticated drag acts to be seen any Saturday night in old city pubs and the brisk bite of urban satire. Mein Herr gawps and the Italian student is mildly uncomfortable. Puzzled perhaps that he has not yet cracked the code. The American rests her parasol and fumbles with a camera. Her travelling companion reaches for a notebook in his backpack. He'd better be a worthy sociologist. Any hint that he's making jotting for some future fiction and I'll have his tripes for supper.

Greg interrupts my conjectures:

Well said, Rose of all but the Third World. What image of India would you suspect this gang'll be taking home with them, eh? Would you, f'instance, say they'll be tough on poverty but a bit tender on getting within touching distance of lepers in that colony on the unfashionable side of Srinagar?

Come now, Reet. Very principled I'd say this lot was. Unlike some as I might name . . . and you can pop that up yer Khyber . . .

Into waspishness, are we?
Must be the heat. So 'ow many
Indians you had it off with this
week, Rosie?

> There was them two untouch-
> ables after tiffin last Monday . . .
> and I must admit to cement-
> ing cultural relations with a shit-
> house wallah before cocktails on
> Wednesday. Oh Reet . . . Reet he
> was so . . . well, so big. You'd
> have thought he'd have been ac-
> tive . . .

Go wash your mouth out with
lake water. You go too far. Shock-
ed 'em, you have. Can't you see
they've been decently reared? Into
plain living and high thinking this
lot is and you have to drag sala-
cious realism into it . . .

> Stop getting at me again. Tell
> you what . . . I won't mention
> sex if you'll let me dress it up as
> politics. That do?

You trying to give the audience vertigo?

> Don't seem to be falling about
> with laughter as far as I can see.
> Come on, Reet. Let's give 'em
> our Ode on Intimations of
> Democracy.

With one scooping movement Greg appropriates the American's parasol. He twirls it above his head and then – as he settles
it on his shoulder – seems almost to reshape himself. He sheds
solidity and his gestures become dainty. Vince – a few paces
from him – diminishes himself until he is so crouched as to
appear homuncular. They sing the opening stanzas alternately.
The final quatrains are treated as a duet which they perform
while circling in front of us.

> Elizabeth Helena keeps to the shade
> Of Calcutta's imperial colonnade.

Her hands neatly gloved and her pigment so fair
(Insulated of course from the overbaked air)
Protected from light by her new lace-trimmed hat,
She ambles to Firpos to sip tea and chat.

Pit-a-pat, pit-a-pat go Ahmed's bronzed feet,
Resembling the undeflectable beat
Of a drum. He makes for the foetid bazaar
Where Gandhi will speak. A rainbow durbar
Of passive resistance that yearns for the day
When sahibs and memsahibs must all sail away.

Elizabeth Helena taps the ferrule
Of her parasol. Ahmed – recalcitrant mule –
Refuses to take to the gutter. A mere
Native reminds her that he was born here.

'Memsahib is the visitor. This teeming land
Is ours.' She pauses. Does not shake his hand.
Yet as his shadow occludes the sharp light
She concedes – before passing – he's possibly right.

The words are set down without any attempt to focus them against the clapping and sandal-tapping which we provided as an accompaniment. Greg and Vince encouraged our participation. My intention in making a quick copy of the words on the back of my road map should be made clear. I've no expectation that they'll be chanted in a classroom but there may still be places where people enjoy a bit of community singing. If there's no tin whistle or mouth organ then percussive clapping to the rhythm of Pat-a-cake Baker's Man will work as well as any.

I'm not the only one who hasn't a free hand to applaud. The researcher – if that's what he is – scribbles as feverishly as an agency man intent on making the next edition. I doubt if his transcription is as accurate as my own, for each time he pauses and looks up he ogles the Italian student. This may be simple friendliness but I doubt it. The younger man blushes and turning away finds me winking at him. Mein Herr hasn't enjoyed the entertainment.

– You should both be ashamed of yourselves. Why must you mock such good people who brought so many benefits to lands that were still in the Dark Ages?

As I could have guessed, Ellen can't resist an intervention.

– What benefits did you have in mind? Bibles in one hand and a few grains of rice in the other?

– So what is wrong with that? . . . If I understand your meaning.

My own contribution goes just a little over the top.

– Let's not forget how our forebears taught them to sow in straight lines through the paddy fields by day and how to sing *The Mikado* in Urdu by night.

The German flushes. Senses that we are beginning to send him up. Vince – as might be expected – can't miss such a cue for a song. He goads the German to anger by flirting his peacock fan as he croaks the words.

> One little maid came from Cawnpore.
> They shot her Dad. She became a whore
> To feed her brothers. She was twelve – no more . . .
> Three cheers for the Raj. Boo Rah.

Greg doesn't do much to enhance international harmony either. Mein Herr strides all of six paces from us. He stands by the corner of the bus where he folds his arms and contemplates the Indus Valley. Or maybe it is the unqualified anarchism of young people today. Greg sinks to his knees and as we watch shuffles towards the outraged business man. When he begins to swim both cupped hands in supplication, we look at one another and wonder if a plea for forgiveness is about to be formulated.

– Mein Herr . . . Mein Herr, please don't sulk. Shouldn't we all learn a little something from yesterday? Please rejoin the human family. If you can accept us then we'll promise to forget your little housepainter . . . well, forgive anyway . . . your little madman with the moustache. There – I knew you'd remember his name . . .

The German turns towards us, his scowl still not quite erased. He's not without common sense and knows he is locked with us by circumstance as surely as if we had been confined to an island. He balances a little humility against exclusion and opts to lean against the rock face not far from me. We sit uneasy – even po-faced – until Vince suggests a game of charades. Greg immediately stipulates that there must be no teams. The idea of such a vicarage party diversion is received with surprising enthusiasm by our random collection of international travellers. The chubby researcher who has sidled with some rapidity towards the young Italian is plainly downcast that his proposal of men versus women is instantly vetoed by a shout. Not that the shout is sufficiently loud for me to miss his question to the Italian. Alberto. Well, having given his name, Alberto moves away. My own suggestion that Vince and Greg should begin is accepted as a counter-proposal. We flop on the shirts and jerseys we've thrown onto the shale. As the actors are about to start, the American woman, who is giving the photographer and Alberto a potted curriculum vitae, breaks off to put a question.

– This going to be the whole story and nothing but the story?

Vince – already squatting in what has to be one of his favoured positions – pulls down the neck scarf which has been covering the lower half of his wrinkled face like a yashmak. Oh I know, yes I know what he's going to say to her now he's pursed his lips like a sugared almond.

– If you want a bedtime story darling, you should have brought a book.

If . . . No. Let's rephrase that. *When* we're safe in Kargil this evening I shall have a word or so with him about that. For the moment I'm content to watch as he very diligently mixes something. A cake? Not another sponge for the Queen of Leh?

Greg – not too far away – bends and straightens as though tending a garden or maybe an allotment. I glance round at the others and notice Mein Herr staring intently. He's probably determined to patch up his self-esteem by winning the game. As I turn my head again to watch the actors, their work mime stops in mid-gesture and they cup hands to their ears.

– They are listening to something?

– Well, they're not making couscous. Sssh . . .

– It's just gotta be bells or singing . . .

No indication from the performers that any of the comments is even remotely on course. They move close to each other. They hug and then look up. They are no longer listening but watching. Greg crosses himself but Vince grabs at his hand almost angrily and replaces it round his own neck.

– It is little men from Mars they're expecting?

– Could be. Why not big women?

– Nein. You are wrong. This is more of their propaganda. These are what you English call gay. We have them also in Hamburg. They are waiting for the police to come to one of their clubs. You will see . . .

– Don't be so bloody sniffy. My kids do classroom mimes like this every other afternoon. They were making scones and digging vegetables, I bet you. It's too early to guess anyway . . .

The actor's mouths drop wide. Both point to some distant happening. Two free hands are raised and clamped against each other's mouths in terror.

– Will you look at that now? What a giveaway. Hand over mouth and eyes popping from sockets . . .

– Ya, ya. You are right. The syphilitic Norweigan painter. Edvard Munch?

– Well, if we're away into the upmarket arts just count me out. I mean, how do I compete in that league? No one like me stands a chance.

Something he's said. Something the chubby researcher has just said. We all agree on that. A word or a phrase he's used has Greg crashing through whatever illusory proscenium arch we spectators have unconsciously erected. He claps the American on the back and dances exultantly round him.

– Now this bit does remind me of my eleven-year-olds doing a war dance.

At this Vince too gallops forward and pulls Ellen to her feet. He kisses her but says nothing. We confer in whispers.

– Pretending to be eleven-year-olds? Can't be that . . . War dance, though, has to be on the right track . . . Your remark about the upmarket arts? Shouldn't think it could be . . . Something you said though. Didn't you say something like not standing a chance? Standing? That's a possibility. Sssh . . . now what are they up to?

Vince and Greg retreat from our loose semicircle and appear to re-establish an Us and Them relationship. They begin to beat the bounds of a second semicircle complementary to our own. Having defined their space they meet at what in more formal theatre would be termed upstage centre. They resume their horrified Munch faces before starting to tear at first their own and then each other's clothes. Lumps are hurled this way and that. The Dutch journalist to my left suggests they may be stripping for gladiatorial combat. Whether this is overheard by the performers is hard to say. It certainly coincides with a fresh development. Still picking at themselves they perambulate the periphery of the grand circle. On reaching the American doctoral candidate, Vince isolates her from her researcher at about the moment that Greg slips between Ellen and her friend. The picking mime continues but now the actors tug first at the clothes and then the bare cheeks and forearms of the audience. We are all involved. Having begun at either end of our semicircle they must finally converge on me.

The Dutch journalist screams with such intensity that our driver drops his cigarette.

– God. Are you all stupid? Can't you see what the story is? It is the bomb. Yes it is. They are dancing the nuclear holocaust . . .

– That is very nice. I take a break, just a little holiday from business where even at the factory benches they talk politics. Now I must have it thrust at me in the Himalayas. Where will this end? In Hamburg . . .

– Well there's no getting away from it is there, Mein Herr? Even here. At least not until they've finished changing that bloody wheel. Why not just watch and find out if these jokers come up with any better answers than the politicians?

The actors break from us and as they retreat dance a *pas de deux* with about as much elegance as a pair of derisive baboons. Greg, sensing that his back must soon be grazed by the rock face itself, flops supine with his tongue lolling. All four of his limbs are raised in the air, reminding me of just how Jean and Sally's baggage mule must have looked when it had slipped on a pass.

We conclude in whispers that a fresh episode has begun. Not that there's instant agreement as to what it might be. Greg could be in an asylum maddened by the bomb. Alberto wonders if he may be impersonating Yossa Asaf resting in his tomb at Srinagar and awaiting resurrection. Mein Herr contends that this would be offensive. Ellen suggests Lazarus might be less contentious. This having been accepted without a vote, she repeats the name so that Greg and Vince can hear. Vince executes three handsprings towards her and she wins the mini prize of a mush apricot. We feel some progress is being made.

Vince grabs the American's parasol once more. Having furled it he marches to the centre of the acting space. As he shoulders it even I guess the parasol is now a rifle. Smart as any toy-town grenadier he does an about turn and brings the weapon to a firing position. Three times it recoils against his shoulder, so in all he's discharged three shots over our heads. This seems oddly at variance with an earlier determination to involve us all. Now we're being warned to keep our distance.

– D'you reckon even Brecht would've pushed alienation this far?

– Sssh . . .

Vince is motionless. Greg stirs and is immediately certain of our attention. He lifts his head then drops it again and throws all four limbs wide on the ground. The Australian finds the tension too testing on a summer's afternoon.

– Reckon he's a welterweight out for the count. I'd split a cold lager with him if I had one. Could revive us both . . .

This provokes some giggling. It's difficult to tell who starts to count Greg out for we all join in. As we reach Five he's sitting. By Nine he's rubbing his eyes. As we shout TEN he starts to shuffle forward from the full shade of the rocks.

– Would that be some parcel he's carrying?

– Who'd bother with parcels or supermarkets?

– In Belsen they still clung to their possessions . . . even a matchbox gave them some identity.

– Why is he turning his scarf into an apron? Is he a transvest?

– Of course not. You're obsessed with stereotypes. He is a woman and that's his child he's hugging through the ruins. Watch how he strokes the baby's legs . . .

– Oh Jesus. Look. His hands keep falling through. There are no legs.

No alienation now. We are all so deep in the horror Greg is inventing with our help, that no one notices the swift transformation Vince has effected.

With shirt collar turned up and the tail spreading outside the seat of his jeans he appears almost formally dressed. This impression is strengthened when he converts the parasol from a rifle to a furled umbrella. The emroidered linen cap he may have bargained for in Leh is perched forward to rest on the bridge of his nose. Others may have laughed at the simple incongruity. I can't know. To me just for that moment he was dressed in the velour trilby and sleek brolly that was dished out with a knighthood to colonial governors.

We rapidly concur on who Vince now represents. He is the carrier of some rare scrap of plastic, entitled to a corner in one or other of those bolt-holes already set aside for the vital bureaucrats without whom no civilisation could survive the nuclear winter. I mutter some of that distinctly so that Ellen overhears. She questions any such definition of civilisation and I'm compelled to tell her I agree.

Vince smirks before waving to the landscape that lies behind us as we sit. He begins to inhale noisily. Is he indicating that the world's air is sweet again? As he smiles at the blue unclouded sky, we exchange obvious phrases.

– Alright for some, eh?

– I'd rather not be there . . .

Greg steals up behind him on tip-toe. No one warns Vince as we might have once – when children – at a pantomine or circus. Greg locks him in a brutal half-Nelson and with one click of the tongue Vince's neck is broken.

Alberto sighs. If there's satisfaction in his voice when he speaks, it is not easy to rebuke him.

– He did not enjoy his . . . his . . . dolce . . .

– Good life?

– Yes. His good life for long . . .

Greg's mime is clear and economical. He staggers back from a quick trip to the rockface burdened with something that is slopping. Water. A bucket of water. Every time the smallest splash is wasted he clucks irritably. His first attempts to kindle a fire aren't effective. Mein Herr with unfortunate facetiousness regrets there aren't any Boy Scout uniforms around so that Greg and Vince could rub themselves together. The Dutch journalist tells him not to be cheap.

Once lit, the fire brings the water to boiling point with unnatural speed. I realise I have relaxed and disengaged myself perhaps too quickly from the action. Greg kneels with his back to us and with Vince between him and the invisible bucket and fire. As I am about to light a cigarette Greg raises his arm. One slicing movement and he decapitates Vince. By craning my neck I am just able to catch Vince withdrawing that plum red nose of his into the neck of his outsize shirt. Greg's back is hunched under the weight of his trophy. He first elevates it, then allows it to plop into the steam and bubbling liquid we have each imagined.

It is impossible for us to know or even guess how many times these two actors have rehearsed this mime. Greg's dance may be improvised as he and we wait for the head to cook. He may hope his movements signifying joy and success put us in mind of recorded precedents. Is he Salome cavorting in her seven veils? Is he Judith after her little triumph over Holfernes? Perhaps he's King David who is on record as being a nimble little mover. Who's to say now whether as Boy David he didn't try out an arabesque or two with the head of Goliath dripping above him? There's no doubt that some of the audience recalled one or all of these incidents as Greg danced.

Vince – or to be accurate, Vince's head – having been seasoned to taste and broiled to perfection, Greg extracts it from the bucket. There's elaborate blowing from North, South, East and West on the delicacy to cool it. Greg pauses a moment to smack his lips. Teeth bared, he rips strip after strip of flesh that is his one source of unpolluted meat. Having gollupped perhaps a dozen mouthfuls he pats his belly and licks his thumbs. He smiles not merely in our direction but at us to indicate his consciousness extends once more beyond his most urgent need. We are offered small gestures of self-abasement and apologies for selfishness before he glides rather than walks towards us. What we are to suppose is Vince's broiled head dangles from Greg's left hand. The fingers of his right wrench choice morsels from it. These he offers us benignly as the celebrant of an horrendous Eucharist.

We edge back from him expressing our disgust. Some have stumbled to their feet and begin to heave as a prelude to nausea. Others – and I am among this minority – back from Greg's hand without regard for our nearness to the crumbling shoulder of the mountain road. I am in the narrowing gap that lies between revulsion and oblivion. Greg has now singled me out and is leaning down until his face leers at me just one breath from my own.

– A tiny wafer, Ian? Chew this in rememberance of all your years of silence . . . all the opportunities to dissent when it was more comfy to play possum, eh?

– No, you bastard. Why me? Why me?

– Have the tongue, Ian. Oh come on . . . maybe it will encourage you to use your own for better things than witticisms over the candied rose leaves and port, eh?

Ellen is calling and the driver is clapping his hands.

– All aboard again. Pull Ian up, Greg. Time for off . . .

But I get up unaided. My only certainty is that I am going to return to my seat unaided. I shall not face the chassis of the bus. Somehow I shall stare at the sky and not look down. Greg and Vince are already converging on me with the expectation that I shall need help. Greg no longer leers and his intention is kind. I refuse gently but do add that I'd be glad if they would keep beady eyes on me. If I should faint or seem to sway they will know when to grab me.

– Hadn't reckoned on political street theatre as a bonus, I must say . . .

– Bloody scary piece to put on for holidaymakers, wasn't it . . ?

– Not as though we could walk out and ask for our money back, eh?

– Bet you won't forget it in a hurry, though . . .

– C'mon, will you Ian? Let's hit Kargil before six, I've got half a reel I want to use up before dark.

Greg precedes me, and shuffle by agonised shuffle, I crawl crabwise along the side of our bus not caring that the heat of the bodywork may be blistering my palms. I am aware that sweat is dribbling from my temples, my armpits, and my crotch.

If I only reach that half-open door somewhere to my right and towards which I do not dare to glance . . . If I can reach that and am then among those who will continue on among the blind bends and frail clumps of wild cornflowers, I will not – when we reach the top of the escarpment – look once at the rest-hut where Daniel and I made love. I will not tomorrow or next winter recall it as anything other than a chance encounter enjoyable just in and for itself. If the shale does not shift now, as I place my right foot on it, I will no longer play possum whenever Miles is mentioned. I will say outright not only who he is, but that I am ready to meet him whether he lurks in the shadow of bushes or confronts me on the houseboat. If no one at this very moment leans from the open window behind my head to taunt me or even playfully urge me to look down, then I will guard my waspishness and direct it only at character-assassinators and those who yawn silently when cruelty is perpetrated against the defenceless. And now – if this is truly the driver's calloused hand still greasy from helping to repair a wheel – I have made it. I have made it alone and will from tomorrow offer affection not merely to the handsome, but to the most ill-favoured. Not from tonight, but from tomorrow and always, I will slide rejoicing into the beds of those more lonely than I could ever be, provided there is honesty in their speech and their glances are gentle.

Vince hauls me into my seat. The driver grunts and offers me a cigarette. Greg in the door-frame of the driving cabin winks.

– Coped with your monster at last, then?

– No . . . No . . . that was not my monster. But it was the last hazardous few paces to his lair.

– A battle to the death with a king-size bedbug in Kargil tonight is it?

– Could be Greg. I think I'm ready for it at last.

A NOT impressively proportioned room. Functional would perhaps be apt. It is the space – no larger than a double cell – that I must share until there is sufficient light for me to repack my toothbrush and my clock. With the first breath I took on entering, I was aware of the acrid whiff from a candle recently snuffed. There's little doubt in my mind it was extinguished while the proprietor was soothing me in the corridor outside.

I consider setting my alarm but decide to rely on the said proprietor's assurance that he will call me at five to five. Should he prove as fallible in that as in his earlier promise, it is unlikely Greg and Vince in their room across the way will trot away to the bus without me. Having tugged off my shoes I stand for a moment listening. Not a sigh. Can he really suppose he'll catch me off guard with a casual greeting as I'm sliding from consciousness? Not one chance that I'll concede him any such advantage. He is awake now and no further than two paces from me in the darkness.

In stockinged feet I pad towards what was advertised by the guest house tout at the bus station as a private bathroom. Even functional would be a generous description. A stained metal bowl in one corner. Diametrically opposite there's a tap from which a lazy dribble can be coaxed to fill what was once a large can for coffee granules. Given patience, sufficient water can be collected either to wash or flush the loo. Before supper – when I first inspected the place for bugs – I discovered my own patience was equal only to filling the bowl for a wash and using it later to sweeten the lavatory bowl.

As I scrape the door across rough concrete, a muffled contralto singing the pop version of a familiar melody becomes more distinct. My private bathroom is as well lit as any alcove in an upmarket restaurant. What with an earlier glance I'd foolishly supposed to be a gauzed window-frame that might offer a glimpse of chestnut trees in the garden, now affords a stage-box view of the next bedroom's shower and loo. This guest house could be starred by voyeurs as a must for any package tour. Hella, our Dutch journalist, stands naked no more than arm's length from me. Confident in her solitude she sings a catchy version of Verdi's Slaves' Chorus that topped the charts in Amsterdam sometime in the mid – or was it the early? – Seventies. She rinses soap from her armpits by the light of three candle stubs and gives fortissimo with *Throughout The World Roses Bloom Now*. Before she reaches what I translate badly as *But They Aren't Blooming For Me*, I interrupt with a tap on the gauze. When she does pause, I repeat my apology that I must piss. She waves with an assurance that I shouldn't worry. As she hears me sloshing water around the pan, she wishes me goodnight with the hope that I'll sleep well. Although I wish her the same, I privately wonder whether I shall sleep at all.

Plainly there can be no further evasion. It is a scene that must be played. To have been conscious of just that and yet pitifully unprepared now it is about to happen is ludicrous. And yet, what point would there have been in telling Daniel I am certain it was Miles ten years ago who sat studying me as I chatted with a ship's tailor at midnight on Omonia Square? How could Daniel have armed me for this? Neither he nor Jean nor Tom, Dick or Harry could have suggested a strategy. I'm on my own in this.

While I am replacing the cap on my toothpaste I at last admit to myself it was I who chose to duck a confrontation with Miles at Aldergrove Airport. Perhaps it is the recollection of my brief involvement with Daniel that strengthens me. Or if not that, then my survival after this afternoon's near disaster. Yet I realise quite calmly this next encounter will have no conclusive resolution. There'll be no corpses in that narrow space between our beds in, say, an hour's time. Exactly why is Miles here? There'll be a glib cover story. That is to be expected. Miles is what Miles always was, plus however many years he's had to perfect his act. But his real purpose here in the Himalayas? To flush that out would be as effective an opening as any for me.

So what point is there in closing the bathroom door gently? I am no longer deceived by bad actors. Miles is awake. I pad back to my single bed and settle myself cross-legged on what I trust is a bug-free blanket. My back is to the wall.

My first interchange after decades of silence with the person I was urged in adolescence to call my brother is so indelible – the inflections and pauses still so vivid – that I think it only honest to set out our dualogue as a script for two voices. This is how it began.

IAN: (*lighting a cigarette and inhaling deeply before speaking. Despite the sweat starting at his nape – of which he is only too aware – he hopes there is assurance in his tone*) Do sit up Miles and let's get on with this.

(*Outside the room footsteps pass the door without a pause. In Room One there is no sound and no movement. Only by gripping his right hand round his left wrist can Ian prevent himself dragging on his cigarette. There is no preamble of simulated yawns or muttering from Miles. When he does reply he meets assurance with assurance and yet contrives to add a top dressing of chilled irony.*)

MILES: We seem curiously sure it isn't Daniel in the other bed, don't we?

IAN: (*torn between relief that the encounter has opened and anxiety that he'll destroy the cigarette between his fingers*) A straight lunge to the crotch for openers, is it? I'm not amazed. You were always a filthy fighter when the referee's eye was elsewhere. It's you Miles, and I know it. That jeep outside among the bushes. It just happens also to be the jeep that's parked on Boulevard Road whenever you're prowling round the house-boat.

MILES: (*clucking his tongue*) Inconclusive. Miles could be here and yet in some other bedroom. Couldn't I be a friend of his – a passenger say – not a little disturbed by your approach?

IAN: (*beginning to smoke more steadily and allowing himself to grip the bedhead rather than his wrist*) Give over, will you? Somehow you sniffed me out and for some reason you've inflicted yourself on me.

MILES: (*laughing a little*) Just as plausibly I might have argued my way into the last spare bed.

IAN: I'm sure you did. But why? I could smell the candle you'd just snuffed as I walked in. You overheard the owner of this flea place apologising that I'd have to share after all with an English guide who happened to have arrived unexpectedly. Unexpected yak's turds. Light the candle, Miles. It must be near your hand . . .

MILES: Surely anything we need to discuss can be said in the dark?

IAN: (*astonished by his own composure as he leans over the side of the bed to stub his cigarette*) Is that so? For once, you superannuated House Captain, it is not for you to mark out the pitch on which we'll play. Light the candle, sod you. I prefer to see what I'm up against.

MILES: As you wish. About to peform one of the great archetypal tussles, are we? (*He yawns – not very convincingly. Having relit the candle he replaces it between the two beds, then eases himself up and settles his head against an inflatable cushion which serves as his pillow*) Still quite confident that I am Miles, then? When did you last meet him? Twenty years ago? (*He folds his arms and grins*)

IAN: (*studying Miles as though ennumerating flaws such as scars and wrinkles*) If it were double that I'd know you. If the We Who Rule England arrogance in your voice had diminished I'd still know you. Who – other than Miles Scaler – would wear a red, white and blue night shirt in the Himalayas? Miles, you're a self-parody. You look bloody ridiculous.

MILES: (*easing back his sleeves to just below his elbows. His arms are tanned and muscular*) Do you think so? There are those with whom I've shared rooms who find me sexy. Or so they've said.

IAN: One should have compassion for the partially sighted. You have my word that you're of no sexual interest to me. Since I can do nothing to advance your career – whatever that may be – it's unlikely you'll pretend to lust after my knickers.

MILES: My interests are not necessarily as restricted as yours.

IAN: You mean some women might find you dishy? I doubt it. Doubtless you find yourself sexy . . . but then you always did.

MILES: (*with a boyish smile of which he is still capable, despite his dawning double chin*) And you did once.

IAN: (*after a moment's pause which he realises Miles will take as a concession*) Briefly. But we change . . . Correction. Most of us change.

MILES: Usually for the worse.

IAN: (*picking up his cigarette pack and – after a second or so – discarding it*) Your conclusion. Not mine. Well now, we're not here for bedroom reminiscences, are we? Fun in other circumstances, no doubt, but . . . here with you Miles, I rather think not. Doubtless you're using this, like every other opportunity, to suss out what you no doubt would call my character defects. It's a trick you've been developing since childhood.

MILES: You think so?

IAN: I know so. Why shouldn't you still be your old manipulative self? Not that I've the tiniest objection to you learning a bit more about me. To be honest, I don't give a bugger if you have a mini recorder stuffed up your night shirt. Now, do tell me . . . just why are you here?

MILES: (*with the mildest of shrugs*) But Ian, you know that already. I'm an English guide.

IAN: (*wagging his index finger*) I know what people say you are. Isn't that possibly based on what you might have told them?

MILES: So what else do you suggest I might be?

IAN: (*laughing easily*) Oh come on! Miles the high flyer has learned to be content with nannying the affluent through a bit of rock scrambling? Now I may have become little more than an overpaid clerk happy among my tomato plants but you'll have to do better than that.

MILES: (*expansively*) Try me . . .

IAN: I shall. A guide must – or we presume he must – have a firm knowledge of the terrain.

MILES: Agreed.

IAN: Ergo this can't be your first visit here. Now here – dear Miles – just happens to be a crossroads between China and Afghanistan. What's more, Pakistan's only a leisurely morning's chug up the road.

MILES: I also studied geography at school . . .

IAN: But what do you study now? Are there political snippets to be gleaned? Or is it dope? Even those who do no more than skim the headlines know where the golden caravan routes begin. What are you into, Miles?

MILES: What was it my father said of you when he was accused of steaming open a letter? You recall the phrase?

IAN: (*too swiftly*) No.

MILES: I think you do. A distressing attack of hyper-imagination. The tendency hasn't disappeared. Just why would I be into anything more than your intimate friend Daniel? Everything you've insinuated could equally well be levelled at him.

IAN: (*with a lightness that he trusts will obsure unease*) Daniel's a romantic. Nothing more . . .

MILES: Well there's no difference between us on that. But

would that necessarily exclude . . ?

IAN: Don't bother to try planting doubts. I haven't forgotten your mean little ploy to alienate my mother. And you needn't assume your injured look. I know that one too.

MILES: (*with some perplexity*) But I have forgotten. I really am sorry, Ian.

IAN: You're not and you haven't forgotten. Nasty little hints about the ticket collector at the station. Mark. You were still trying out the Miles Scaler syndrome then. Alienate. Isolate. Control. You're better at it now.

MILES: I fail to understand . . .

IAN: Then I'll spell it out. As far as Daniel is concerned you can shut your tight little mouth. I always did think it prim as a puritan's arse.

MILES: (*having registered Ian's anger and seeking to stoke it with the flicker of a smile*) I'm sure you must feel so much better for having said that. I quite see all this is splendidly cathartic for you but is it getting us anywhere?

IAN: (*calmer again and ready to pretend as politicians do that his anger was only a pretence*) Where exactly should we be getting? As we parted last time I yelled after you words to the effect that I didn't give a fivepenny fuck what you did with your life so long as you didn't tangle with mine. Well, I wouldn't alter a syllable of that except to take account of inflation. Neverthe-less – since you've weasled yourself into my room – I intend to find out why.

MILES: (*shrugging his shoulders before replying*) I can only repeat – will that get us anywhere?

IAN: I shouldn't think so. Well . . . not in any sense that you interpret it. I'm happy to consider this as an exchange of views.

MILES: So be it. I'll concede I could be in India doing just a little more than ensuring some business bore doesn't have a cardiac arrest while in my care. (*He inspects his thumb and then removes a fleck of mud from beneath the nail*) In return . . .

IAN: True to form, Miles. Never invest without being certain of a return.

MILES: Surely. In return you will no doubt allow that your involvement with Daniel wasn't, shall we say . . . an unfulfilled friendship? The days – or rather the nights – of the yearning urnings are over, are they not?

IAN: Think what the hell you like. It's of no relevance to you.

MILES: No? Let us suppose . . . this of course is hypothetical . . . that your seduction of Daniel resulted in more than physical satisfaction. That you experienced a tumescence of radical idealism. Now if that were so . . . not an idle supposition . . . then everything you said in a double bed two hundred kilometres up the road might well be of interest to me.

IAN: To a trekker in climbing boots?

MILES: Don't be obtuse Ian. You wanted to play for real.

IAN: To you in your patriotic nightshirt, then?

MILES: Just so.

IAN: (*moistening the underside of his top lip with his tongue*) Fascinating. Not that you should be some kind of a part-time spook but that you should use your time here to check on me, I mean . . .

MILES: But how could it be more than supposition? I've not glimpsed Daniel since you both left Srinagar . . .

IAN: You'd no need to. One of your friends, though (*considers who may have risked cramp and a chill crouched under the bedroom window*) . . . the hunchback who sold me cigarettes? Too busy in the kitchen, I'd have thought. Ah ha . . . *la belle Hélène*. The Parisian school teacher. If that is what she was. A busy little doubt-sower, whatever else. You would have been proud of her . . .

MILES: (*refolding his arms and hugging himself*) Warmer, Ian. I find myself in an indulgent mood. It's possible we may not meet for another twenty years.

IAN: I'll make damn sure we've no need to. You and all you embody will be engraved on my memory with acid.

MILES: How nice of you to say so. And will I be as sharply outlined as Daniel who – I do admit – retains that vulnerable downy look I once had . . .

IAN: (*shaking his head and smiling*) I'm not rising to that one . . . Wait . . . yes . . . Hélène's lover. Yves. Of course. Yves. He's one of yours. Watching like you. Brooding on the edges of conversations and assessing. Poor Yves shivering under the window sill. I just hope he got his rocks off on our pleasure.

MILES: He described you as rather comic.

IAN: No doubt his privations sharpened his tongue.

MILES: He tells me you were conducting what might be termed a teach-in on sexual politics within seven minutes and forty-five seconds of climax. All those fine sentiments you've only ever had the guts to confide to your tomato plants suddenly welling up. Sad, eh?

IAN: (*unperturbed*) So Yves is also here on the tax-payer, as it were? A spell for at least two of you here in the sun. Who's paying? NATO, is it this time? Or the CIA? MI 69 perhaps? Who cares anyway? (*He leans forward*) But it should be exposed. Not to my tomatoes either. I mean I should go and talk to an editor when I get home.

MILES: Do. But who would publish it? Anyone who didn't throw you out as a paranoid would make certain such a yarn never appeared. The cruel reality, dear Ian, is that we never need to censor editors. They do it so smoothly themselves.

IAN: Oh come on. England's England.

MILES: Indeed it is. And public recognition is sweet to middle-aged editors. Sweeter for their ambitious wives. So which of them is going to risk some anticipated chocolate medal by printing your deluded ramblings? No, Ian, we can talk openly without fear of being called to account.

IAN: (*not replying until he has lit another cigarette and blown what he hopes will be a smoke ring towards Miles. No smoke ring forms*) Shall I tell you what most disgusts me most about you? What nauseates me even more than the sight of the starving picking among the stinking refuse in Dehli?

MILES: You intend to do so. Not that it will add to the aces in your hand.

IAN: Maybe. You disgust me Miles because you exude a stench more cloying than any I've experienced in India. It's your incomparable talent for promoting suspicion and mistrust.

MILES: And this can only be a bad thing?

IAN: Without any doubt. Unless you're watched . . . more than that . . . unless you're understood and guarded against . . .

MILES: But do go on.

IAN: Unless all those things and more Miles . . . then – with the help of your like-minded pals – you'll divide and rule us all.

MILES: At least your penchant for vivid abuse hasn't faded with the years. A little more controlled perhaps. Well, now. The concepts underlying what you've just been putting so colourfully could very well account for my interest in you. My marginal interest . . .

IAN: I could hardly hope to merit more.

MILES: Had you let me finish – I'm secure enough not to be riled by abuse, by the way – had you let me finish, I'd have added that as any kind of threat you're not worth a moment's unease. None of the bickering little radical sideshadows you've flirted with over the years could ever be a threat worth discussing.

IAN: Just a little bit over-assured Miles? Some disquiet underneath all that firmness perhaps?

MILES: Not at all. Think back. You and your ticket-collector running round youth festivals on a lambretta. What did that ever achieve? What did solidarity with the students of East Europe ever do for you, eh?

IAN: Well, for starters, I didn't glide swiftly from puberty to middle age.

MILES: (*folding his arms behind his head and looking quizzically at Ian*) Now that is quite remarkable. Your allusion to middle age I mean . . .

IAN: Go on then. I'm not trying to hide from it . . .

MILES: That is not the question. It's the form middle age may take. Yves, for instance, did wonder if you might be experiencing a menopausal upsurge of social conscience.

IAN: I hope you had a good laugh. You seldom did, as far as I recall.

MILES: It's not a matter for laughter. Let me be plain, Ian. Although I find you irritating as a bedbug I wouldn't wish you to begin gnawing at the social fabric immediately you set foot on English soil.

IAN: (*discarding the cigarette which is beginning to burn his fingers. He does not care where it lands*) Whatever my intentions might be, you'll get no advance warning.

MILES: I can't do fairer than advise you not to run round our crumbling inner cities with a revolutionary tract in one hand and the other on some window-dresser's willie. (*Ian is beginning to lick his fingers*) You might suffer more than a cigarette burn.

IAN: (*thumping his hand down into the blanket as a fist*) And say I did? Surely that would delight you. I'd be making exactly the moves you've decided I should make.

MILES: I fear you've lost me.

IAN: Piss off. You and your cleancut pals are obsessed with the tactics of dissent. You sit in your club chairs playing endless games to outwit anyone who disagrees with you. Anyone who dares to pop a head over the parapet to say so . . .

MILES: Unless you're feeling the heat, I'd suggest it's you who is becoming obsessive . . .

IAN: I'm sure you would. Miles, we owe each other less than nothing but can I urge you to sit quietly and alone for just one hour here in the . . .

MILES: But I often do.

IAN: And just let it trickle across your mind that it could be possible we're heading at an imperceptibly slow rate towards something that – elsewhere – we'd call an banana dictatorship. Surely you'd have reservations about that. You can't be insensitive to everything but power.

MILES: (*selecting a boiled sweet from a bag and throwing one at Ian who leaves it beside him on the blanket*) Have one. They're soft-centred. Like you. Poor Ian. Now so long as you rant away – entertainingly, I'll admit – you'll have no hassle from those who think as I do. You theatrical pals Greg and Vince appear to have dredged up a number of half forgotten hopes. If it gives you satisfaction to voice them . . . so be it. Carry on raising laughs at Speakers' Corner on Sundays, then drag back as many men as that coarsening bag of bones of yours can manage.

IAN: Very generous of you, Miles. What's the catch? There must be one.

MILES: Indeed. Should your listeners begin to applaud what you say, that would be very different. How do I put it? Things might become a little more troublesome for you . . .

IAN: And there we have it. Democracy defined for us by Miles Scaler. I take it Greg and Vince are destined for some future mishap if they too start to influence their audiences in a tiresome way?

MILES: Do credit us with some sophistication Ian. Money's tighter by the year now. Why pay *agents provocateurs* when actors will flush out troublemakers for free? Greg and Vince are doing splendid work. Time they had a grant. There's a contact of mine from army days working for the Arts Council who . . .

IAN: Their performance this afternoon might have distressed even you. The nuclear holocaust and its aftermath.

MILES: I rather think not . . . from what I heard. One does overhear chatter at supper tables in these small towns. Perhaps it was the international flavour of the occasion that affected you. Your old dilemma popped up once more, did it?

IAN: My turn to say you've lost me.

MILES: The question is whether you've lost it. The old hogswash of liberal humanism, I mean. Is Ian Prote still as ready as he was in adolescence to put his pals before his country? That is what I was implying.

IAN: (*slowly untwisting the sweet wrapping*) You're thicker than I thought.

MILES: If I smoked I'd have one of your cigarettes.

IAN: I should have remembered. Even a boiled sweet has its price.

MILES: Can we go back to the central issue? Are you suggesting I'm too thick to note some unsuspected patriotism in you? Do tell more.

IAN: Miles, you really are a top-league wanker. My country could never be sold.

MILES: How thoughtless of me. You are a citizen of the world. One of the teeming millions united by deprivation despite frontiers. Except you are not one of the unprivileged, are you Ian?

IAN: Your irony has the period touch of a cavalry charge.

MILES: I'm listening.

IAN: Then get this the first time and get it good. Who could hope to buy or sell my England? What's the bidding price for the Thames on a windless afternoon in May? Can you quote me the current rate for crowds enjoying a funfair next Bank holiday? They're about the only commodities I've shares in.

MILES: (*slow hand clapping*) Very colourful. You've not lost your old touch. Should have been a poet you know. Do forgive me, Ian, but you did say about the only commodities.

IAN: (*plumping up the meagre pillow and sticking it in the small of his back*) Hoped you'd not overlook that. I also have the right to dissent. My own tiny share in something dearer than platinum. I'm well aware there are those intent on whittling away at that.

MILES: Do you think we keep our brains in our boots? Do you imagine you're the only one to realise the imperial game is over for us? It's no breach of classified material to tell you we know as well as you that our tight little island is slithering towards a tourist and sardine economy . . .

IAN: But who shares out the sardine rations, eh? No prizes for guessing who'll get the fat ones and who'll have to be content with tiddlers.

MILES: But all will get something, Ian. No point in provoking unrest, eh?

IAN: Give 'em bread and circuses.

MILES: (*smothering a yawn that is – for once – genuine*) Why this self-imposed misery, Ian? No one is going to pay you to revive Spartacus. Why not stop all this cultivation of dissent? You could be a very positive asset.

IAN: (*amused*) What's on offer?

MILES: Whatever you wish. How's about a pleasant set of rooms in one of the more mellow universities? It could be fixed. No one would object to a discreet curly-haired scholar.

IAN: (*incredulous*) You'll need to do better than that.

MILES: True. I was being insensitive. About the curly-haired lad, I mean. Daniel was rather an aberration, wasn't he? You were always more partial to a bit of the rough and ready, as it were. Your ticket-collector and now this boatman.

IAN: Don't tell me you're stumped. Note the cricket reference.

MILES: Got it. A sinecure on some artistic sort of committee with a sturdy working lad thrown in. The Russians fixed Burgess up with a musical peasant, didn't they? How could we offer less?

IAN: In return for what? You're a mite uneasy about me, Miles. You want my silence. I wonder if you envy the small scrap of courage I have.

MILES: Now that's nicely phrased. Care to give me one instance of this small scrap of courage?

IAN: Sure. The courage to try although I may be wrong. A willingness to make a fool of myself . . . to slide on my arse and still laugh at myself. To pick myself up again and trek on. In short, Miles, risking hazards you'd never dare.

MILES: Useful qualities. Isn't it curious . . . we're in no way blood-related yet we might very well be twins.

IAN: The idea appals me. What can you mean?

MILES: All this detestation for me you've been mouthing. (*Consults his watch*) I must be brief. Making a five o'clock start.

IAN: Get on with it then. I'm fascinated.

MILES: (*unwrapping a second sweet. This time he does not offer one to Ian*) You shouldn't imagine I'm going to launch into that old Freudian line about sibling rivalry. That's light years from what I'm suggesting. I do actually suspect that under all you've been spouting this past half-hour there's a bedrock of horror in you. Oh yes. You're petrified you may resemble me. Hold on, old son. Laughter's not your most dependable shield in this one . . .

IAN: Miles, you *are* laughable. Resemble you?

MILES: Just let me finish. I don't doubt for a second that you conceived this little chat of ours as an almost mythological meeting. Your grounding in the poetry business and so on. Right. I'll put it in those terms. The real monster you feel you have to come to terms with – if not destroy – is not me at all.

IAN: Oh no?

MILES: Very much so. It's part of yourself. The Ian you have presented to the world for a couple of decades now. For all I know or care the Ian you have learned to live with quite comfortably. Ian Prote the conformist. Sad, eh? Very sad. Nevertheless . . . to be practical . . . it would form the perfect cover if you cared . . .

IAN: (*irritated*) You are a steaming shit.

MILES: (*grinning*) I would accept realistic.

IAN: (*genuinely angry*) I don't need you, Miles, to tell me what I might have seemed to have been to myself or any other bugger. What I am now is relevant. What I will be. Nothing else.

MILES: (*laughing*) A hit at last. And to score, all I've needed to do is voice a reproach about your easy lifestyle these past years. That's the weak point in your defence, Ian. All the questions you've opted never to ask yourself . . .

IAN: (*calmer again through the anticipation of a morning in which he will walk unafraid*) But which from this instant I shall.

MILES: Brave. It could jeopardise your well-cut suits. You looked quite trendy at Aldergrove, I thought. Must have been ten years ago.

IAN: Planning a discreet lunch with my boss? Am I to be eased out?

MILES: Are you worth it? My expenses have just been cut. I should think you'll do it for yourself if you act on all these tiresome notions . . . then what would happen to your exotic holidays where you can brood on the injustices and sufferings of the world?

IAN: (*on surer ground now*) Still the House Captain, aren't you, running us all with offers of threats or treats? Which hand will you have, Ian? There's a stick in this one and a carrot in the other. Don't fret about me. I'll find the means to travel. Not planning on restricting passports yet, are you?

MILES: Not at all. To be honest it might be preferable . . . well
. . . less expensive . . . if some of your ilk quit England for
good. As it is, I suppose you'll be able to carry on patronising
– I do beg your pardon – to go on furthering international
understanding by getting local boatmen to open their legs for
a pack of duty-free fags.

IAN: (*irritated to realise that he is tiring*) Nothing I can say would
make you understand.

MILES: Try me.

IAN: (*leaning forward so that Miles wonders whether his own
exhaustion is obvious*) You said that before. No, I'll not be
drawn. Even though you've insulted Bashir and sniggered at
me. And I won't bother to throttle you when you do sleep. If
you say that's ungentlemanly, I'll counter by reminding you
that your own friends' technique has · never been very
Queensberry Rules when faced with equal opposition. And
that's what we are.

MILES: Are we so? I take it you mean on a personal level?

IAN: What else? You've got the money. You've got the
network of contacts which you're sure will allow you to
conscript whoever and whatever.

MILES: But not you, eh? Or any of your dissenting friends?

IAN: Spot on. So you must hunt me as tenaciously and just as
warily as I must elude you, Miles.

MILES: You phrase it very dramatically. Such adversarial
terms.

IAN: You're a cool bastard. I'll give you that. There's no other
way for me to put it. You are the hunting dog for all those
who not only want to stop the clocks but to turn the hands
back. Some of us dare to think otherwise. And I shall go on
doing so whether you offer me an easy sinecure or reduce me
to a cup of rice on a cardboard bed by the Thames or in Delhi.

MILES: We'll see.

IAN: And so shall I. You're welcome to live in yesterday, Miles,
but don't try casting me for a walk-on part. The candle's
guttering. You bore me. I must sleep.

MILES: But I'm enjoying this. We must arrange to meet again.

IAN: Don't count on it. Go and play your Prefects' game in
some other flash point of the globe. It's comforting to watch
how you have adapted your talents to the late twentieth
century. I understand – I really do – how much happier you
would have been serving the Raj.

MILES: (*settling into his blanket*) It was your parents I seem to recall – not mine – who were here in India some decades ago.

IAN: Don't try rewriting history, Miles. Keep to the facts. My parents dared to have supper in the Twenties with an Indian musician's family. Two days later they were given a ticking off about losing caste. Hints of a passage home if the indiscretion was repeated. Now who shopped them, I wonder? Maybe even set them up? Were Miles Scaler's pals always lurking in the shadows, I wonder?

MILES: I assure you, Ian, I never knew that.

IAN: Since deception is your bread, butter and jam don't expect me to accept that. I do just hope your report of this little encounter is accurate. (*Also settles down as the candle fizzles*) Wouldn't want you pushed out without a pension, Miles. Mind you . . . we might use your expertise . . .

MILES: (*alert instantly*) We?

IAN: So you are tired. Didn't think you'd fall for a little joke like that.

MILES: (*after a silence during which Ian is sure he can hear sounds that are suspiciously like the grinding of teeth*) So where do you see yourself in twenty years, Ian? A tiresome old man haunting protest meetings in half filled draughty halls?

IAN: Bit incautious of you, Miles. Doesn't that presuppose you won't be strong enough by then to forbid all unlicensed gatherings? And who are you to say the halls won't be full and overflowing? If your sad little vision doesn't become reality, it's you who might be doodling over the tomato plants. Incidentally, where do you live?

MILES: (*drowsily*) I have an apartment.

IAN: But where? Let me guess. Somewhere anonymous on the fashionable side of the river?

MILES: Keep guessing.

IAN: Of course not. That wouldn't fit with your Spartan self-control would it? I have it. I have it, Miles. A pad in that same leafy suburb where we were schoolboys. That nice Mr Scaler who works in the City somewhere. Goes jogging every morning through the very streets he knew as a lad. Always busy at weekends too with a dedicated little group of conservationists. They've restored the Victorian bandstand in the riverside gardens. And a good thing too. Got rid of the undesirable elements who used to loiter at dusk. Now Mr Scaler's friends have started to rebuild those amusing little cottages near the church to house the deferential poor. We locals call him Mr Miles now. Getting a bit jowly he is. Can't understand why he flourishes a riding crop as he walks through the Council Estate, though. There's those as say if he strides much faster he'll meet the nineteenth century coming towards him.

MILES: (*distantly*) Fuck off.

IAN: (*sweetly in the darkness*) Sleep easily, dear stepbrother. Your secret's safe with me.

MILES: (*sighing with irritation*) What now?

IAN: I know the object of your secret lust.

MILES: Not you, for sure.

IAN: I'll live. So will the rest of the world.

MILES: (*muttering*) Can't you stop babbling and sleep?

IAN: Relationships with others are beyond you, Miles.

MILES: Indeed?

IAN: You are – and always have been – too deeply in love with the taste of your own sperm. Always will be.

MILES: (*yelling*) Fuck off out of my life, will you?

IAN: (*laughing*) At last. Words that I've waited years to hear. Far sweeter than I Love You. Sleep with that thought. (*He continues to laugh – each time more softly – until he sleeps.*)

SOME OF us watch alone. Others – Sally and Jean for instance – in pairs. There are also family clusters such as that which surrounds an Arab trader. Intermittent spokes of light reveal unsuspected viewers crammed in shikaras and the distant swimming-boats. Bashir might be among them.

I wonder if the OOOH, as rockets blossom, and the ensuing AAAH, as a last floret explodes, are common to all firework watchers or whether the Italians, Swiss and Spaniards, who stand near me on the steps of a papier maché factory, have just picked up the habit from Anglo-Saxons. As the novelty fireworks scud and skip from the water's edge, I peer left and right to the margins of our group. Miles does not appear to have joined us but I've no doubt he's watching from the boat itself.

My beer can is empty. Unless I've overlooked a waiter circulating somewhere in the darkness, there'll be no replacement for another ten minutes at least. The figure stepping gingerly towards me is no waiter. I don't need the glow of a catherine wheel sizzling on a poplar trunk to recognise Jean. She wears a plain cotton tunic over her jeans and her hair hasn't lengthened perceptibly in the week since we last talked. The harsh magnesium flare of the fireworks highlights for me her own distinctive beauty. Not that her royal blue tunic set against the tan on her arms or even the smear of fuschia lipstick that she wears is evidence of an attempt at conventionally winsome looks. By the yardstick of commercial advertising she is as plain as I am. Though we have not discussed the matter, I'd guess we have both long since understood that whatever attraction we may have for others must be based on honesty in speech spiced with occasional wit.

– Been too bloody busy, Prote, since you got back to have a natter with us, I suppose? How's it all been – or aren't you going to let on to a couple of down-under Kiwis?

– Come on now. Didn't I wave to you both across our floating palace half an hour ago? Maybe I can join you when we're back on board. You do both look as comfortable on your cushions as a pair of suffragettes in a brothel. Anyway, you must have noticed I was nattering to that Indian family from South Africa most of the time.

– Who is he? We saw them arrive this morning. He doesn't look short of a penny.

– Just as well. D'you know these neolithic clowns in Pretoria actually tried to insist he send his son off to some university they reserve for Coloureds? The guy had to bribe the family doctor to certify the boy has asthma before they could apply for a place locally. What d'you reckon to that?

– Well, the system there stinks but you shouldn't slobber too much compassion on him. First – if he's a businessman – he's sussed that the more bureaucratic any system becomes, the more easy it is for common sense to sniff out a loophole. Two . . . he'll certainly have been stacking good dollars under the floorboards for years at the expense of those Boer farmers. That said, let's get on to more important matters, like I could do with a bloody beer.

– Sure. Isn't discrimination important too?

– Great to hear you getting passionate about it, Prote. Well . . . about the theory, anyway. Sal and I were saying only this afternoon it might have done as much good for you as a person to have got involved with Bashir right here in Srinagar, instead of eloping with the ever lovely but unquestionably white Daniel . . .

– You're an evil bloody pair of witches.

– Bit strong Prote. Bit strong . . . Where's yer evidence?

– Don't imagine I didn't hear you both laughing down the passage this afternoon. I know damn well you and Sally were sniggering behind the sunblinds as I flopped into Bashir's boat.

– Just innocent delight that things were working out for you. Don't tell me you didn't enjoy your excursion through the everglades?

– We did.

– That's fine then. You do realise you were followed? That other pom – Miles what–his–face – had the hotel shikara brought round five minutes later. Some kind of peeping Tom, is he?

– You could say so. He wasn't away long?

– Funny you should say that. Back in ten to fifteen minutes I reckon.

– Long enough . . .

– For what?

– Long enough to bribe a couple of fishermen to annoy us. Everytime we pulled into a shady backwater they'd come punting after us.

– You're joking. Is he kinky or something? Reckon he fancies Bashir?

– No, he dislikes me.

– You knew him back in England?

– We grew up – I didn't say matured – side by side. His father married my widowed mother.

– Stepbrothers?

– No blood – except maybe bad blood – relative. His own mother had died.

– So he buggered up your afternoon.

– Not a bit. We tantalised 'em twice. Third time Bashir knew what to do. Tied up the shikara among some reeds. I talked to myself while he slithered away and when they moored just within peeking distance he dived under and capsized them.

– Ace. Then you and Bashir had it away in the mud?

– Kinky. No. We got the hell out of it and shook them off.

– Must hear more sometime later about Miles. I didn't come hopping across the shit to hear about him really. There is something I should tell you.

– Nothing to my advantage I'll bet.

– Too bloody right Prote. But not one damn syllable will you drag from me till I've found a beer.

We tread carefully by the light of fireworks between the goat's turds and some slime I'd rather not define, across Poplar Island to the gang plank of our party boat. The Indian trader and his family have remained on board and are watching the display from the open stern. All the musicians are resting before they resume entertainment with what Jean and I wager will be yet another twenty-four verse ballad. With choruses. We collect two cans each from the corner bar and are instantly presented with our drinks bill for the evening so far. Jean explodes:

– Some bloody party. Back home in old world Wellington we expect the booze to be on the house. The amateur mafia that runs these prison hulks must have skimmed enough from us this past week to pay for all this and still clothe themselves till next season . . .

135

– Will they be seeing you both again? Next year I mean.

– Here? You're joking Prote.

– Well . . . India then?

– Life's too short. Sal and I fix on a different spot each summer. Scandinavia next. We discussed it this afternoon. At least the sanitation will be better than this.

– Cheers. And cheer up. Think of it as a few more tales of old Kashmir for winter evenings when you're home.

– Too right. Now listen Prote, you wonder of all the gay world. Sal and I have a small bet on about you . . .

– You're pausing for me to make a wild guess? How's about . . . yes . . . did I or did I not have Daniel in a mountain cave surrounded by rampant stalagmites?

– That covers bet number one.

– Jean. If number two involves the exact location of the plumbing at the critical moment, you demean yourself with an unsuspected coarseness. Drink up. The next lager's on me.

– As far as who did what to which, you can die with your secrets, my love. That was *not* bet number two.

– I'm tense with anticipation.

– And so you'll have to be until the end of this evening. Or until something that has to happen happens. No more clues. Meanwhile can I cadge another load of this gnat's piss for the Shepherdess? Daniel still convinced we're both lezzie, by the way?

– I just may finally have got him to accept you were devising a game to tickle his fantasy. Mind you, I wouldn't care to vouch for what he might be thinking this very moment.

– Fair point. Amazing the games we all devise, eh? Listen. Sal and I will stand you a farewell brandy back on the hulk when this apology for a piss–up's over. If you'll join us. And if we're right – reference back to bet number two – you'll be needing one.

Improvising a pair of weighty castanets with her two unopened beer cans, Jean moves away in search of Sally. Before I've swallowed a couple of pulls at my own lager, they reappear recrossing the gang plank with other guests ambling in their wake. The show is over. Sally waves to me as she moves on into the busy lounge. Plates of Kashmiri food are being set out among the cushions and the room buzzes with chatter. Language barriers and reticence have been breached by the shared experience of the entertainment.

I am not over-hungry. These Kashmiri specialities of shredded lamb pummelled for hours before appearing as stewed meat balls don't tempt me. They've been appropriated from Persian cuisine anyway. Figuring that there'll be ample time to help myself to spiced salads and some fruit when others have eaten, I wander back across the gangplank and linger on the prow. Two boatmen are plunging whittled poles into the mud so that we can be towed by a power-boat round Nehru Island and on towards the hillside, where lights from the Maharajah gardens flicker through the trees. To starboard, three or four shikaras follow us. Once again I wonder if Bashir might be paddling one of them. Does he hope that by repeating to himself often enough that we shall drift away again tomorrow afternoon, it will happen? I could cable London and plead sickness. An extra week with Bashir would be good and a stomach upset would be a readily accepted explanation. Less bewildering than any contention that I had been charmed by a boatman perfectly formed from head to thighs, but then – adapting to a life passed almost entirely in a shikara – completely underdeveloped, with the legs and feet of a twelve-year-old. Less bewildering, too, than a few syllables on a cable form suggesting my karma dictates that I should stay.

Shall I – in London – think equally of Daniel and Bashir? Even posing that question, I realise I've given priority to Daniel. I hope it is not because he like me is European. That would be banal. Racist. Is it then because Daniel and I shared more than a couple of hours under the willows? Were we responding to some quality each of us had to offer the other – a hunger long unstated that surfaced when the occasion occurred? Having been made love to by a friend rather than grouped by some fumbling stranger, Daniel can move easily now in the silence of a Himalayan evening. I have exorcised for him the shadow of that cousin to whom he so obviously wished he had given himself. Ian Prote, too, can travel blithely now, without giving the brush-off to those whose physical imperfections or intellectual shortcomings have hitherto cast them as poor understudies for bronzed team leaders. Miles' ghost is laid for me.

And how shall I think of Bashir? There's his carefree and uncalculating affection certainly. It's a safe prediction that he'll be either by the houseboat or the landing-stage in the morning when I cross to search for an airport scooter taxi. I shall decline the management's shikara and insist that he ferries me. Whatever the number of staring holidaymakers, I shall hug him and give him my two best shirts as a present. He has asked nothing of me. Would not allow me to stand us a couple of lemonades. When I produced a note as we slowed by a soft drinks boat, he laughed and waved me away before raising the sacking on which we'd made love. His shikara lined with rupees. Maybe he'll use my shirts as an extra lining. It's pleasant to suppose he might wear them and think of me this autumn. The summer is breaking here too. Three willow leaves float below me and there are spots of rain on my arm. I turn and move to the shelter of a striped canopy.

The young woman in the door-frame wears a white boiler suit. Her black hair is styled as my own was when I was in my mid-twenties. Her eyes, more than her mouth or nose, remain memorable. They shine like two immense toffee apples from the shadow of the canopy.

We do not need to introduce ourselves.

On the BBC Third Programme an anthropologist is giving a talk. His name may be Dr Glyn Daniel. His listeners certainly include a schoolboy named Ian Prote who lies on a quilted eiderdown and who has one arm round a young ticket-collector from Richmond Station. The speaker tells us that farmers scattered in North Finland need neither post-boxes nor telepones. Although isolated by midwinter snowdrifts they can communicate telepathically with the few neighbours that make up their world. A wordless rendezvous can be agreed at midnight by the birch tree that overhangs some tiny frozen stream. Any farmer can then trudge off with unassailable confidence. He knows his friend will be waiting.

This reminiscence occurs as I move towards her and is succeeded instantly by a doubt that I have confused telepathy with precognition. The realisation that I have indeed done so causes me to smile at myself. This may well be interpreted as a welcome by the petite figure who watches me steadily. I have no means of knowing how nearly she resembles any photograph Yves and Hélène implied they had been shown. I asked for no description of her and none was offered me, yet I need no third person to introduce us. This is Charlotte.

– You're Daniel's wife. I suppose you must have arrived in Srinagar while we were away in Ladakh?

– Very good. I am Charlotte but I arrived only yesterday by the bus from Jammu. They told me the Englishman – the one who went with my husband – had returned at lunchtime. Tell me Mr Prote – how is Daniel?

– Ian, please. How's Daniel? Well . . . very fit, Bubbling. It's for you to say his usual bubbling self.

– He is always . . . Vivacious? Yes? . . . Vivacious when he is away in Ladakh or Zanskar.

– He did say that he'll be back here sometime next week, but then you possibly know that already. So who was it told you I was here, Charlotte? The two New Zealand women, I expect.

We are now facing one another with our backs supported by the door lintels. She has something waiflike about her. It is of course the Minelli look, superimposed on the sallowness of a South European complexion. Waiting for her to answer, I note a cool humour in that toffee apple glance.

– Why should that be so important? Well, perhaps it is to you. You must have noticed, Ian, that if a guest loses even some sunglasses on a boat like this all the other tourists and the staff become involved in a hunt until they are found. These places are like a village. If I am staring at you by any chance, it is because you are not the man I expected you to be.

Daniel cannot have been in contact with her. Who then can have told her anything about me? Neither Sally nor Jean would have had any motive for doing so. They are not manipulative. Miles? Does she know him? Has he sought her out? Unless . . . unless . . . Daniel's dead cousin? Is there a photograph of him on every wall of their Parisian apartment? Does the ghost of the lover who never was grin over the shoulders of a seemingly ideal couple? Could be I'm being measured against him.

– Why should you expect me to be anything, Charlotte?

– It would have been more honest of me to have said that I always expected this would happen. I mean that one day I would meet just one of the friends Daniel has spoken of . . . that this conversation would happen.

– I'm sure we're at cross purposes, Charlotte. Daniel was kind enough to offer me space in his hired truck on the road to Leh. I don't imagine I shall see him again, though to be truthful I did scribble my London address on a sheet of toilet paper and fold it inside his backpack. I doubt if he'll ever find it.

She does not offer me a cigarette. The slim fingers she cups round the frail Indian match are quaking just a little. Would she attribute that to the chilly cross-breeze if I asked her? I suggest instead that we might move inside. She shakes her head, then blows a smoke ring and looks beyond me at the carved pinewood panels that surround the door.

– Daniel will have told you we met at Primary School? Yes. Of course. Two bright well-fed infants from homes with books and holiday places along the Loire. In many ways Daniel is still that lively infant and I am the sister he never had. If you are thinking all this is disloyal to my husband, I would also say he is the brother I never had. Nearer my own age than my blood relatives.

So then . . . has Daniel never asked more of this attractive woman than companionship? Have contemporaries at the college disco and the local supermarket accepted without the faintest question mark Charlotte and Daniel as an enviable couple – at once compatible and complementary? Is she troubled by his professed interest in other women? Even if she is, there's no logical basis for her to assume her husband and I have been anything more than companions in a battered truck.

– Why should you feel the need to tell me this, Charlotte? Nothing Danny said leads me to doubt that he loves you. I hope I'm not stirring anything if I tell you he did say yours is a very open marriage.

She accepts the second cigarette I shake from my pack and lights it from the stub of the one she has half smoked. When she has inhaled, she lowers her left hand so that it cups her chin. With her smallest finger she scratches the edge of an eye tooth.

– You have a very charming manner, Ian, but I do not find you . . . disarming? I think that is the English word. After all, there is no reason why we should not be quite honest with each other on this matter . . .

– In this matter . . .

– Oh, you are a teacher?

– For a year or so . . . but that was centuries ago. The symptoms still show when I'm uneasy.

– And now you are uneasy? Because I am a woman or because I am Daniel's wife? There is no need, I assure you. Were you uneasy in the mountains? Not with the glaciers, I mean, or those terrible paths that are always subsiding. I mean were you uneasy with Daniel?

– Never. Everything was so incredibly beautiful. I mean the landscapes were quite like walking on the moon. There was no unease. Daniel and I talked a lot but that wasn't because we were shy . . .

– That is interesting. I had always thought the English would be too shy to talk after sex. Well . . . do go on. Tell me what two male lovers say in the half hour after their first climax.

– Now just one tiny moment Charlotte . . .

– Oh no. Not even one. I would like to hear how your sentimental friendship – no that is schmaltz in English – your romantic adventure began . . .

I smoke my cigarette and say nothing. She gives me only a few seconds.

– Very well. *I* will tell *you*. You were planning a quiet holiday here by the lake. Daniel – exuberant as he always is when meeting a stranger who interests him – enticed you into conversation. Which did he offer first? Was it a trip to the tomb that the locals swear is Jesus Christ's? Or was it a picnic and a swim? These are his alternatives but it depends always on the weather. And then there was just by chance a spare seat next to my husband in the truck? Correct so far? I think so. From the look you are giving me, Ian, I suspect you would like to burn me in the square at Rouen like Jeanne. I am not a witch. How could I know the routine Daniel has established unless he had used it so often? You are, my friend, far from being the first man to have shared my husband's bed . . .

The shale is slipping and my foothold's gone. No matter how tight I close my eyes, my base is crumbling and the bus is out of reach. I am falling . . . falling . . . falling headfirst into a ravine. Daniel's words and Daniel's kisses batter my head and limbs like cascading baggage and pathetic mementos.

The beer can in my hand must buckle soon. If I apply more pressure to the back of my head the scalp must split and bleed and meld me with the door-frame. I try to review the scenario Charlotte has outlined. She could have learned of our picnic from the hotel staff who packed our luncheon-box. Or from that bastard Miles sniffing for information. Any of the lurking waiters might have heard us discussing a visit to the tomb if the morning shower had continued. No. Either Charlotte is harvesting hearsay to check Daniel's truthfulness or their marriage is not as open as he implied.

– Charlotte. I know nothing of any games the two of you might invent in Paris to pass your winter evenings. It *is* my business if you try to involve me and I resent it. Daniel and I became good friends and that's something I'll remember with gratitude. Now – I mean right now – I'm hungry, and I guess you may be too. If you'd care to eat here I'll go in and fetch you a plate and a cushion.

Only as I'm piling our plates do I become aware that I'm sufficiently angry to be using the serving spoons as knives which I'm jabbing into the salads. I have been outmanoeuvred by Daniel. All his ingenuous boyishness was an act and I unwittingly have followed countless others onto the stage of his travelling show.

Charlotte has slid onto the scrubbed deck at the base of the door-frame. She accepts the cushion I offer without speaking. I squat opposite and open beer cans. She can continue for I shall not.

– I cannot understand why you do not admit what I know already. Do believe me, Ian, when I tell you that there is always such a man as you whenever Daniel leads a group into the mountains. If I am hurting your pride I am sorry, but you are not a child as I think some of the others might be . . . Thank you for the salads but I am not hungry. Why not eat and let me talk?

– What more do I need to hear?

– If you will be patient you will understand why I am glad it is you I have met rather than those who preceded you. Now . . . I told you Daniel is still very like that little boy I sat next to at school. Just nod. Don't speak. When you were with him didn't he manage to make you feel sometimes that you were also fourteen again? . . . Exactly. That is just what he was when he first went to the mountains in France with his cousin. And yet with you there is a difference. While you were finding a cushion I began to define it. Perhaps you think I'm going to say it is that you are older than I expected? That is not the point. He has shown me photographs of the others.

– They are just clones of his dead cousin?

– Not at all. They do not look as secure as you do. Confident is the word I am looking for. They were no threat. I could laugh at two lonely schoolboys cuddling together in the mountain darkness without women. By the way, Daniel talked ceaselessly about women? I'm certain he did. They don't disturb me either. But you do. Will you tell me one thing?

What is there left to conceal? She is not bluffing so why should I? Ian Prote, who for only the second time in his fucking life wished to offer everything, has been had up, down and sideways by this woman's husband. Had indeed. Poked, screwed and conned rotten by the most astute games player in the Himalayan league. Miles is a Sunday amateur by comparison. Charlotte shall hear every syllable she wants and does not want.

– You kissed him, Ian?

– Sure. And he kissed me. Often.

– He has never kissed the others.

– Or so he told you . . .

– Do you imagine I don't know when my husband is lying?

– If you say so, Charlotte.

– I do say so. And you still have not told me what you talked about. Afterwards . . . or did you hold each other like Hansel and Hansel under the *tricolore* on his sleeping bag? I don't think it was like that.

– No, it wasn't. I don't know what he'll tell you but – as far as I remember – he asked me if I am homosexual. That was before . . . well . . . before. Later I said, or anyway inferred, that to me a homosexual is a shrivelled fruit stone. I am gay. That's not just a nicer word but the flesh, the taste, the skin and the bloom that surrounds the stone . . .

– To be less poetic, you are what you are without regrets or shame?

– Precisely. Now if that threatens you in some way I'm sorry. Are you worried he will write to me? Try and slip across to Dover for a weekend?

– No. Not at all. We shall see what happens in Paris this winter. I must hope it will be just us usual. Daniel will select a photograph he has taken this season as our New Year Card. He is very good at lettering and mounting . . .

– If you say so . . .

– I did not intend any *deuxième* sense. This year as always he will address a card to each of his conquests. No doubt you will be added to the list, Ian. I should tell you that our arrangement is for Daniel to let me stick on the stamps and post the cards.

– But you forget to do so?

– Is that relevant? In any case, Daniel and I have always agreed that we do not give our summer lovers any address in Paris. The posting or not posting is of no consequence is it?

Except perhaps to those whose romanticism has been stirred by Daniel's attentions in other summers. That – it must be conceded – is not Charlotte's concern. There are a few moments to reflect on this and to surprise myself by how cool, even distanced I am already when discussing Daniel. I find myself thinking of Bashir.

As I wait for Charlotte to return from the bar, Miles strides past me out of the drizzle. He certainly did not come with us on the party boat when we first set off on this evening's junket. Ever the schoolboy sleuth, he must have joined us from one of the shikaras while we were moored to watch the fireworks. Who could doubt he's been lurking on the prow behind the pile of food churns and beer crates to overhear our conversation? The smirk extending from his eyebrows to the cleft in his chin confirms this.

Charlotte offers me a lager can. Her hand is steadier. I hope she'll be less eager to score points.

– I suppose you are wondering why I stay with Daniel?

– If the companionship suits you both what's it to do with me? For all I know there may be family property or money or whatever that would complicate a divorce . . .

– That is perceptive. I think we have balanced things well. Companionship combined with our own private lives. Would you say that is a self-indulgent luxury, Ian? Do you see us as the pampered but doomed bourgeoisie?

– Who am I to judge or offer absolutions? Sure, you and Daniel are lucky. You have the option of playing winter games with each other, wearing the masks that suit you best. But then you've used this summer to work with -what was it – deprived children? Who am I to say if that's guilt or frustration?

– And you indulge yourself, Ian, with attractive men in strange beds around the globe.

– Sure I have the luxury of choosing what to do with my life. If the politicians go for the big bang it'll close the options for us all. Rich and poor . . .

– And what do you do for bread?

– That's unimportant Charlotte. It's finding time between the breadwinning to be a person . . . and distancing oneself a little. That's important . . .

– And a luxury in itself. Even for us Westerners that is diminishing . . .

– And yet no one can finally legislate against the option to dissent. Many try. Tell me Charlotte. Have you noticed Miles – the English guide – taking an interest in our conversation? Don't turn yet. He alternates between brooding into his beer and keeping an eye on us. Is he reckoning we'll end in bed together? You do have to admit it would complete the triangle . . .

– Sometimes Ian, I think I am unfortunate in my choice of

men.

Thick-headed Ian Prote. Charlotte has made the journey from Delhi to be with Miles, not with Daniel. It's a script that works on the political level. On a personal level it's flawed from the start. If she sees through Daniel, then she must see Miles for what he is. He's touring ham compared with her husband. Miles with every step and gesture rehearsed is no more than a grotesque parody of the outdoor hero. He is Biggles plus. Huck Finn on stilts, beside whom Edmund Hillary would appear – to the imperceptive – a mere gnome . . . Is he an Olympic performer on the double mattress?

– Miles is still watching us?

– Uh huh . . .

– Then he is wondering if I am telling you that I met him this afternoon by the landing-stage. He said he had been watching you with a young boatman but he expected you back soon.

– He tried to break up my afternoon. It backfired on him.

– But not before I learned enough to guess about your holiday affair with my husband . . .

– Bit brief to be called an affair, Charlotte.

– Well, anyway, whatever it was. Miles and I talked because, you see, I did want news of Daniel. The mountains can be dangerous as you know. Miles seemed very miserable about something . . .

– Yes?

– Do I really need to tell you we went to his bedroom? Oh Ian, it was all so funny in a sad way. I need not have bothered. Miles could not get – is it in English an erection?

– It is. I hoped you're not suggesting all these hearty heroes have difficulties with women? Not hinting they're basically homosexual, are you?

– Oh no. Miles is not what Daniel calls gay . . .

– What Daniel calls . . . ?

– Your face looks like a mask that has been left out in the rain after a fête. You let yourself be taken in by Daniel's acting more than I thought. I tried not to smile when you related to me your conversation in bed. Perhaps you should have studied his eyes to see if he was laughing. You thought Daniel knew nothing of such a world?

– You mean in Paris too . . ?

– I have learned when not to ask questions. But Miles is still watching. He is very different. I wonder if he needs anyone, Ian?

He is Narcissus pushing through the crowd to find his own face perhaps. Certainly he was not searching for mine . . .

Suddenly I can place Miles in a context where he would be at home.

Welcome to San Francisco and the Badlands Bar on Castro. Correction. Not the Badlands. Sadlands. Heavy rock paints dark stripes across the gloom. Should anyone – i.e. me, i.e. you or the very next person you may meet – be skilled enough to fashion a clockwork clone of Michelangelo's David and push it through the louvred doors, not one of these drinkers would react. No hombro in sombrero, nor holidaying clerk in a ten gallon, nor overpumped student in a dime-store hard hat would blink. Our Miles should be among these waxworks high in the Sierras of their fantasies and champing gum. And should the aforesaid David dare to offer him or any of them the time of day, why then, from lips opened no wider than a pinhole he would hear:

– Piss off. You're standing between me and my mirror.

– I assure you, Charlotte, he'll not be searching for mine. Seems the party's breaking up. There's our landing-stage. You'd be welcome to join us for one last beer. Sally and Jean – the New Zealand women – are buying . . .

– You are a kind man, Ian, but I shall say No. Would I be wrong to think you can also be a hard man in bargaining for what you want?

– Charlotte. I do not want an affair – either condoned or clandestine – with your husband. Should you both find your-selves in London . . .

– No. That would mean a return invitation to Paris. No, Ian. Not because of what your English neighbours would think . . .

– Oh come on. It's not like that now . . .

– But it may become so again. I read some English papers too . . . I was going to say that for us to become involved with you would complicate the games Daniel and I understand. The rules exclude a third player.

– Alright. I'll see you in the morning before I go.

– I shall take my coffee in my room. Goodbye Ian. Travel safe, as the trekkers say.

– And you. Sleep well.

As I kiss her lightly on the forehead, she does not look up at me but beyond to the verandah of our houseboat decorated with ropes of shielded candles. The light shower has finished but there is a breeze flurrying the lake.

I regret having chosen to sit with my back to the water. The houseboat staff pass in relays behind Sally and Jean, distracting me as used cooking pots are carried from the party boat towards a narrow strip of turf that leads to the kitchen. It is impossible not to be aware that washing-up has started among the reeds no more than a few paces from where somebody – Charlotte? Miles my auto-erotic shadow? – is pulling a loo chain. Very consciously I avoid speculating whether it is vomit or excrement that's spreading through the water.

Sally offers a cigarette. Since I've only one left in my pack I pretend to have smoked too many for one day.

– So then? Worked out bet number two yet?

– Well . . . it has to involve Daniel. Since Jean and I crossed out who did what to which, there can't be much left. You tell me.

A mound of cushions topples from a waiter's arms and cascades around both women.

Jean leans forwards thumping the table with her fists while Sally laughs.

– Jesus. This gang contrives to make its guests feel less welcome than a whore at a christening. Don't try putting racism on me, Sally Iveson. I'd say as much back home and well you know it.

– Know why I'm laughing, Prote? Jean's beginning to miss her bloke. Time we turned for home . . .

– Will you shut up, you daft bitch?

– See what I mean? This is how our holiday bit always ends. Her feller loves her partly because she's a feminist. Can he make her accept she needs him once in a while? No more the hell can I, come to that. Got any special feller yourself in London?

– No. Because I choose not to. Don't imagine I'm turning to God or Nature because they can't let you down. I take my own path. Amazing the pleasant people one meets at crossroads or overnight stops. And that – before Jean says it for me – brings us round to Daniel, doesn't it?

– Too right. But first may I publicly thank Sal Iveson for her sisterly support so understandingly expressed. She'll get as much from me next time she's groaning on her bunk with the trots.

– Do us a favour. Go and book a call to Wellington, love . . .

– Maybe. Later. Anyway Prote, you appeared to be spending half this evening chatting up Danny boy's wife. Haven't you got all the answers now?

More to the point, these women have. How early did they guess? As Daniel built a fable about them both on the swimming-boat, were they – as I thought – speculating about us? Could they at that distance have seen more clearly how Daniel was looking at me more than I myself did, being interested only in Bashir?

– Listen, both of you. When we were guzzling campy oranges at the Maharajah and you began winding me up about Daniel, I told you the truth. He wasn't even in my sights. I fancied Bashir. Finish.

– I'll buy that. Tell you for why. Sally's eyes weren't concentrating on the middle distance while you were speaking because I'd just given her a sharp come-uppance. Your friend Bashir's just ferried along behind your back. Maybe your interest isn't one-sided . . . Not got something set up for tonight, have you? I mean, let's not keep you . . .

The last few phrases I hear over my shoulder, for I'm up and leaning over the verandah rail. There is no movement in the unlit backwater that reaches beyond our bedrooms. As I am about to reply I catch the sound of a tiny plop in the darkness. It could be Bashir feathering his oars, but common sense suggests it is more probably a fish snatching at some morsel best not thought about. Both women are giggling as I sprawl in my cane chair once more.

– You two evil witches having me on again? Okay. You've had your fun. I was about to reveal that as Danny and I churned on through the mud up and over the Koji-la pass, it did begin to occur to me that he might fancy me.

Sally opens her hands sufficiently to enclose, say, a potter's wheel. She shapes a lighthearted fiction. As she concludes we all laugh, for they know that I know that they know.

– There you were. Two healthy men footloose and fancy-free and alone on the highest point between us and Leh. Mateship was the name of the game, of course. Let's not forget the nights were cold as a glacier at midnight. So who could say now exactly when or why you found yourselves cuddling up? Except

– Prote old sport – wasn't like that was it?

– You seem to have plotted it out move for move. What can I add to anything you're certainly going to tell me?

– Naughty. See, Jean? Told you his pride'd be bruised. Looks like these beers are on us. Cheer up. Sure we nattered about

Daniel when we got back from the Maharajah. Wasn't difficult to spot that daring Dan was eager for a bit of the other. So long as there were no witnesses to shatter his image.

– Like I said, I hadn't an inkling until we were over the pass and into the Drass valley. Don't tell me you're going to give me the female intuition routine?

Jean intervenes.

– That's all shit, for starters. My bloke in Wellington's better on intuition than Sal and I together. Aren't you forgetting that in this instance we were on the outside taking a cool stare at the both of you? If you hadn't been dreaming of sliding Bashir's knickers down, you'd have been able to study Daniel over the drinks too. You were going to travel next to him in that ten-tonner if he had to drag you there by the pubes, mate . . .

– Obvious as that, was it?

– And more . . .

If this has been their wager, I find it trifling. Although I enjoy their company, a blend of exhaustion and boredom begins to seep through me. I enjoyed what appears to have been a game with Daniel, though all the umpires seem to agree I lost on points. That's their view. Though I'm not wearing my wrist watch, I'm certain it must be close on midnight. A post mortem on any game tires me.

Sally notices my withdrawal of interest. She has said something to the effect that because it's late she might as well give me their complete reading of the episode. I pick up on her exact words when she's as far as:

. . . the question in our minds has been who he fancied on his trip in July and just who he'll be zooming in on in a week or so, when we're all home and frying the chips. Bet your best shirt on it, Prote. It'll be a feller. All that crap of his about being fascinated by intelligent women is so threadbare you could throw apricots through it and still miss the fabric. He's into men. Charlotte's from Paris too, isn't she? She's no village idiot. Did he marry her because she didn't care?

– She knows, Sal. I could see her giving Prote a hard time while we were crunching the lamb bones.

About half a dozen of the hotel staff have perched like bulbuls on the verandah rails or on the nearby tables. They are listening to all we say. When we have become irritated by this or when we have no more to discuss, we shall go to our rooms. This one used table-top will be wiped and then they will blow out the candles and turn off the coloured lights around the dining-room doorway. Now they are leaning in from their listening posts more eagerly than Jean and Sally, waiting for me to comment.

– Charlotte told me more or less what you'd guessed. She stays with him motivated by . . . well . . . sisterly love. It was a childhood match and there's built-in companionship for them both. As for Daniel and the way he appeared to have tricked me . . .

– Appeared? Now come on, Prote . . .

– Will you listen? There was a trick within the trick and that I did not lose. Put it this way. To me the tanned explorer had seemed always a figure I could never become . . . fearless . . . independent . . . dependable too . . .

– A thumbnail sketch of Miles the latter-day Empire-builder.

– Thanks a lot, Jean. Well below the belt though you weren't to know it. Miles may appear to have those qualities. He's a fake concocted from a squash court, a Savile Row tailor and a traditional gents' hairdresser.

– Jean and I reckon he might be some kind of a spook . . .

– Probably.

– I called him a walking wrist-job, Sal Iveson. Am I right, Prote?

– Certainly. To get back to Danny . . . and to me . . . and those qualities I mentioned. Maybe I've aped them too and Danny took them for real. It's possible. Miles after all deceives many people, I'm sure. So . . . Danny saw what he wanted to see in me. The embodiment of a cousin he once loved, as it happens. We've met. Made love. Now neither of us needs to strut. We can both walk easily in future. Does that make any sense? To be honest, I'm tired . . .

– Bit heavy on the metaphysicals but I get the drift, Prote.

– More than I do, Jean. What's the future, Ian?

– Who knows? I guess there may be plenty to keep me busy in England. But I'm glad I've been here.

– When do we get the line about the mountain solitude having had an effect on you, despite all the piss taking we had from you about trekking?

– He'll put everything down to Daniel, bet you Jean . . .

– Sure, the combination of Ladakh and Daniel has been some kind of a catalyst, I suppose. Promise you won't giggle?

– We're not likely to see you again, so why not tell? Confessions to a stranger are still popular.

– My last word then. It's brought home to me at last something that should have been dazzlingly obvious years back. There's no perfection in any lover. In the darkness the most sunripened hero whimpers as much for a shoulder on which he can depend as the cripple in a bed-sit or the chorus boy in a crowded bar. Which means right now I'm thinking of Bashir and I wish like hell I didn't have to go in now and pack.

– A month or so with him might be good for you. Didn't I say as much earlier, Sal? Shall we cable London for you and tell them you're prostrate with something vile and tropical?

– No. There are things to be done. Things Miles may not think important but I do. If I stayed it would be harder. Who'll take a bet I won't come back, though, some other year?

Inevitably we find ourselves swopping addresses. Even as I scribble mine I know it is little more than a meaningless convention and I'm pretty certain both women feel the same. Sally hugs me and then – as I kiss Jean's cheek – she breaks away.

– Hey, Prote . . . give Bashir a hug through your window for both of us, will you?

– Piss off, Jean. I know damn well you were winding me up. I may see him in the morning. Now I really must sleep. Overnight to Paris tomorrow and – just before you say it – I'm not into checking the phone book there.

There's little space left. Some must be used to state that the I who has made this journey through Kashmir and Ladakh is Ian Prote, a character not entirely coincident with the writer who has evoked him. Even words on a page cannot clothe him with any substance. Prote breathes only with the cooperation of the typesetter and your eyes that now skim these lines. Miles would probably be happier if Prote did not breathe at all. He'd quite delightedly stuff Ian into a file – even some prison or mental ward. Miles' world would certainly be less tiresome if Ian Prote could be numbered – 82391 would be as good as any – and thrown into a dusty basement.

So what would Prote do, having blown a kiss to the two New Zealanders? To discover that, one must return to the first person singular and follow him.

Having bolted the door of my room, I hurry to the window. There are no shikaras to the left or the right or on the still water below. No Bashir.

In the bathroom I piss, then wash my face and strum my teeth while deciding that there really is no urgency about packing. The spare hour after breakfast will be more than ample time.

I drop my shorts to the floor and – picking them up to fold them – hope they will fit as easily next summer. As I wander across to the bedside table I drop my head and inspect my thigh muscles. A small vanity, but it pleases me to check that I don't yet wobble as I walk with the jelly roll of the middle-aged.

Something animate brushes my leg as I reach for my alarm clock. I freeze and instantly recall an obscene flying beetle that scared everyone witless as we waited by the carousel for our baggage three weeks ago in Delhi. Whatever the creature is, it must be found and trapped in the waterglass. If it is not out of my room and into the lake, I'll not sleep. With any luck I'll not place my foot on it, although the light from my bathroom is pitifully weak.

As I pick up my travelling clock, my leg is brushed a second time in much the same spot. The corner of the bedsheet flickers. In the shadow Bashir is smiling at me. Whispering Hello. Jean and Sally were not joking. He did row past the verandah and has somehow opened my window gauze. I drop onto the bed to hold his hand.

– Bashir. You must go. No. You must go. Soon.

But not too soon. And if I come back to Kashmir next year or ever it will be to seek out Bashir, not Daniel. Or Bashir's son, not any lad Charlotte and Daniel may adopt some winter. Even this. The world of monosyllables and mime that Bashir and I construct is plainer – more to my taste – than dancing through the maze Daniel devises to shield himself from the simple appetites of friendship.

Bashir pulls himself to a sitting position to hold me tightly by the biceps. I run my right hand firmly through his shoulder muscles and turn his head so he must look at the window-frame through which he has slipped in. With my left hand I extend a line from his nose through the darkness towards the gauze. He frees his head and shakes it until I sigh. He is not leaving. I cup my hands behind his ears and we laugh softly into each other's faces before we kiss.

– When the sun comes up Bashir goes. OK?

He has not understood. I use my bedside torch to sweep a small beam from the table in an arc above us. I tap my wrist and then he laughs again.

– Sun come. Bashir go. OK.

For the first time since leaving London I must set my alarm. It had better be for five o'clock, or the hotel staff will be swarming to prepare their own breakfasts or trampling the daily wash in old zinc baths outside my window. Their disapproval means less than nothing to me, but Bashir must stay and live among them.

It is as I peer at the clock-face by the light of my torch beam that I first notice the lettering. My own name has been printed between the alarm dial and the spindle on which both hour and minute hands turn. Chinagraph on the card. I twist the clock against the torchlight, suspecting there might be guidelines for the lettering but none are apparent. Either it is the work of a professional artist or a template has been used. Turning the clock one last time I spot fresh scratches in the paint that expose a glint or so of metal. This amateurism contrasts oddly with the calligraphy. A professional, but in a hurry. I have no doubt whatsoever that the dial cover has been prised up by Daniel's omnipurpose knife.

Yet when did he contrive to do this? To imprint if not on me, then on my property some souvenir of himself? Not in Kargil, for sure. There we slept in a dormitory with four others. It may have been five.

I turn the alarm key, divided between a hunger for Bashir and a compulsion to run a fast replay of that day at the rest-house on the pass. There could have been no opportunity for such loving handiwork as this while I was in the latrine. Daniel certainly humped our baggage into the double room. I keep my own gear locked. Unless he also picks locks he could not have got at my clock.

. . . *Something I had to do took longer than I thought* . . .

As I sat waiting for him in the village square he was tracing my name. So much for Charlotte's contention that the only gift he ever offers his lovers is a New Year card that is never posted. Is it unwise – a regression into sentiment – to be touched by Daniel's gesture of affection? Should I presume I have been singled out when very possibly it is his habit to inscribe some memento for every man he's bedded? There could be examples of his artistry in bachelor apartments – or family households too – around the globe.

Bashir is waiting and there will an opportunity on the plane to think through Daniel's motives. It will be pleasant – there's no denying it – to wind this clock in conference hotel bedrooms or when I am alone at home. The wretch need not sit grinning, though, on winter nights. He should not presume that winding it with some lover by me, I'll superimpose a sunburned nose and cornflower eyes on any other face. As, for instance, now. Bashir is Bashir.

I slide beside him, pulling down the cotton sheet. The bathroom light stays on, for I need to see him as I touch him and watch his eyes as he holds me. He's taken a shower somewhere this evening and his skin is scented with rosewater. Not – I discover – under his arms or crotch. There is the sharp tang of salt in my nostrils and on my tongue. My fingers speed casually through his curls and I murmur that he's been using a shampoo. He recognises this word perhaps from the bold print on a sachet and bares his teeth in a row of peeled almonds as he grins. When I run my tongue along their even surface he responds by tucking his feet round the back of my calves.

There's no sadness in his eyes. Their greyness echoes the mountains that will be silhouetted beyond my window in a few hours. He does not expect to discuss or plan anything. We look at each other for some moments and then he lifts my hand to replace it, so that my fingers – pointing down – touch the film of hair below his navel. And then he smiles and whispers:

– Love.

I recall how reticent I've always been in all the beds I've shared to shape this tiny abused word. Now, as so often elsewhere, my only response is a smile.

– Love.

Bashir whispers a second time. Daniel's features frail as a paper mask whisk in front of me. The mouth beginning to shape my name seems distorted. I hear Miles running tap water in the next room. Has he been at his exercise in front of the dressing mirror? Somewhere out on Lake Dal two ducks break the surface with their wings and squawk on their way over the roof. I hear in their noisy chatter both Vince and Greg urging me to quit the audience and dare to join the show. My lips close on Bashir's as I murmur:

– Love.

Recent fiction titles published by GMP include:

Tom Wakefield
ISBN 0 907040 80 2 (cased)

The Discus Throwers
79 9 (pbk)

Considered by many critics to be one of Britain's most original contemporary writers, Tom Wakefield has been widely praised for his depiction of the humour and pathos of human relationships. His latest novel continues in the same vein, charting the progress of five everyday figures who react against the social conventions that have shackled their lives. "Wakefield is an accomplished narrator; detached, witty and knowing" THE TIMES. "It's refreshing to come across an English novelist who knows exactly what he's doing and does it resoundingly well" PETER ACKROYD.

Rufus Gunn
ISBN 0 907040 95 0 (pbk)

Something for Sergio

Neil's journey across South America leads him into many adventures – sheltered by Indians in the Amazon rain forest, initiated into voodoo rituals in Rio, befriended by political refugees in La Paz. The goal of his quest is Sergio, the passionate love of his schooldays, but their eventual reunion has an unexpected twist. "Considerable quality as a writer . . . a gift for selecting the telling detail and projecting it with telling power" MARTYN GOFF. "A thoroughly good book . . . funny and interesting" IRIS MURDOCH.

Graeme Woolaston
ISBN 0 907040 81 0 (pbk)

Stranger Than Love

A winter morning in the backstreets of a small English town; in these greyest of circumstances, Eddie and Rick first become aware of each other . . . "A gritty, sometimes frightening, always compelling novel about the relationship that develops betwen a gay man in his thirties and a strikingly attractive youth who is slowly revealed as a queerbasher. That the book is neither judgemental nor slickly sentimental indicates the level of success the writer has achieved in his handling of an unusual and immensely difficult theme" MISTER.

Alex Hirst
Almost One

ISBN 0 907040 69 1 (pbk)

From the pages of an old journal, a young man recaptures key moments in his personal odyssey, and through this route makes a provocative examination of the fantasies and realities of gay men today. "Displays an intelligence, gift and style so lacking in the majority of gay male novels. Read it" TIME OUT. "Passion seethes in bursts of writing that are not less than beautiful. A work that aims to push the limits of expression, a type of literature that explores truths, and questions their existence" SQUARE PEG. "A jewel of a poetic novel with a multitude of overlapping images and meanings. The images are haunting and the epigrams are incisive" BI-MONTHLY.

Simon Payne
The Beat

ISBN 0 907040 70 5 (pbk)

Friday night in a city park and a young man is found battered to death in a public toilet. But this is no simple case of queer-bashing. Six strangers hold the answer; they alone know what really happened that evening – when the intended victims suddenly struck back. "Crisply written, entertaining and thought-provoking. Simon Payne is a writer worth watching" BRITISH BOOK NEWS. "Compelling reading" GAY TIMES.

Martin Humphries
(editor)
Not Love Alone

ISBN 0 85449 000 0 (pbk)

The first in a new series of Gay Verse contains new work by British and American poets, including contributions from Thom Gunn, James Kirkup, John Lehmann, Felice Picano, Carl Morse and Ian Young.

GMP also publish a wide variety of books in other areas, including art and photography, biography, drama, health, history, humour, literature and politics. Our full catalogue is available from GMP Publishers Ltd, P O Box 247, London N15 6RW.